SEASON

of

LOVE

CATHERINE LEE CLAY

SEASON

of

LOVE

ATHENEUM 1968 NEW YORK

FOR
LUCY ELIZABETH & JOHN COLES
WHO MADE POSSIBLE MY DELIGHTFUL
VISIT TO THIS WORLD

SEASON

of

LOVE

chapter
1

THE WORLD that Laurel Carlton knew that summer was the
plantation in Virginia—thirteen hundred acres of red soil,
and red gullies, and woodlands, varied with countless
streams and springs. On one side it was bounded by the
leisurely meandering creek with its boulders, its shallows, its
deep swimming holes, its cliffs covered with mountain laurel
and hickories and oaks and ferns, with trailing arbutus and
wind flowers, with columbines and rich green moss and crisp
gray moss. May suckers and catfish and bass swam in the
creek, and schools of minnows danced around them. The
creek was beautiful and infinite in its capacity for entertain-
ment.

Fertile fields and orchards surrounded the house, and tenants farmed some excellent bright tobacco land on the east side of the plantation. But more of the land was good only for wild dewberries and broomsedge, for pines and thickets, for wide red gullies decked with shining bits of white flint. For Laurel, the treasures on the place were numberless. There were black walnut trees, chinquapin bushes, hazelnuts, hickory nuts. Occasionally, she found an Indian arrowhead in a furrow or under a sassafras bush. She loved to pick the big, blanket-like leaves of the plantain and hold them against her face.

A hundred yards back from the big road, sat the house in a grove made up mostly of locusts and cedars. It sat comfortably in the yard back of the big lawn. It was a white house over a hundred years old, with a steep shingle roof and dormer windows, and two wings in the rear. It had a small front porch with square white pillars, and a double front door that was never locked. Clustered in the back were outbuildings of all sorts, the most important being the little house occupied by Great-uncle Cam when he chanced to be there.

Laurel loved the house and the plantation with a love so deep and instinctive that she never put it into words. It was just there like the sky and the land and the mammoth conical boxwoods that bordered the yard on the West.

It was on a day in early June that Laurel stood at the yard gate and watched her parents drive away across the lawn, bound for Lynchburg, New York, and Europe. She couldn't believe it, yet there it was happening before her very eyes. It was as though the world were moving out from under her. Of course she had known for months that they were going, yet the actual event had seemed always in the future. Now that the future was the present, it was incredible.

Mother, very correct in her white shirtwaist and dark blue suit, turned to wave. Papa swung his new white panama gaily in the air. Only the driver, Billy Watt, did not turn.

With his old black hat on the back of his head, he drove through the big gate and out into the road as nonchalantly as usual. Then she saw him lift the reins and raise the whip. Soon she could hear only hoofbeats on the hard red clay road. In that moment devastation struck her. She turned and pressed her face against the paling fence.

"What's the matter with you?" demanded the newly installed housekeeper, Mrs. Prickett.

She couldn't answer. She was too shaken by her wild nameless grief.

Gan put an arm around her. "Don't, child. We are all here with you."

But not Mother and Papa, she thought. She felt that the world had ended, and the odd part of it was that she hadn't known that she would feel this way. Through her grief, she was shocked at herself.

"I declare," said Mrs. Prickett, "folks would think you were three instead of a big girl of fifteen." She looked disapprovingly over the tops of her glasses.

Still Laurel did not answer; she stood staring down at her bare feet.

Chris was already chasing a butterfly across the lawn, his net outspread in the breeze. Roy, her younger brother, was headed purposefully toward the carriage house, where she knew he was trying to devise an engine for his red wagon. She was amazed that they could be so callous. How could they put Papa and Mother out of their minds so quickly?

Uncle Walter, who had come to spend the summer, announced tersely, "Grass is out of hand on this lawn. I'm going to turn the cows on it. You kids keep the gates shut." Rolling up his shirt sleeves, he strode off toward the stable.

Her seventeen-year-old cousin, Edgar, leered at her. "Baby!" he taunted.

She struck at him, but he sidestepped, and she nearly lost her balance.

"Now, now," Gan murmured. "Let's go to the house, dear,

5

and shell the peas for dinner."

She walked stiffly beside Gan up the brick walk, scarcely conscious of the green June all about them.

"My," Gan said, "so many roses this year!"

Laurel glanced blankly at the two great pink climbers that made a cascade of blossoms from the steep shingle roof to the ground on each side of the front porch. Ordinarily she delighted in the roses, even scattering handfuls of petals over her bed at night, but now she could think only of her woe. No one else cares, she said bitterly to herself, they all go on just the same.

She was not fond of work of any kind, but today there was a sort of solace sitting beside Gan on the back porch, shelling the peas that Brindy, the cook, had picked right after breakfast. She knew instinctively that she was not ready for the summer, that it was not going to be like other summers. She had the strange feeling of being older and younger at the same time. It was a thing you couldn't tell anybody, a thing you couldn't really understand yourself.

She could hear Mrs. Prickett bustling about the kitchen, talking with loud authority to Brindy. Brindy's answers, if any, she could not hear at all. She knew Brindy did not like interference.

Gan was talking casually, not bothering to exact replies. The June apples would soon be ripe. Tomorrow they must pick more dewberries. Even though Mother was away, they must can a hundred quarts as usual. A hornet landed hopefully on the edge of the pan, but hornets, Laurel knew, didn't like peas. They preferred very ripe apples or pears. She watched it fly away again. Long ago she had learned that things like hornets and wasps did not disturb you if you paid no attention to them.

When the peas were shelled, Gan took them into the kitchen herself. Laurel sat on, staring absently out at the poultry yard, where three white Peking ducks were guzzling

6

happily in a pan of water. It crossed her mind that they would be delighted to have some crawfish caught fresh from the branch, then she reminded herself that such a meeting would be far from delightful to the crawfish. Today she did not choose to wrestle with this problem. She felt too lost and lonely to extend her sympathy to the outside world.

On an impulse she got up and walked to the old red cupboard at the end of the porch, where she had shut away her dolls. She hadn't played with them for a long time now, but she still loved them. She opened the door and took out her favorite, Mary, the one with the painted china head. She was holding it tenderly, gazing into the unswerving blue eyes, when a raucous laugh made her jump. She whirled about. Edgar. He had a habit of sneaking up behind you like that.

"Dolls!" he jeered, "playing with dolls. You're too old for that."

"None of your business what I do."

His dark eyes gleamed. "Say now, you're no kid anymore." Before she could guess his intention, he had jerked the doll from her hands and hurled it across the back yard into the poultry yard, where it struck a flat rock. The lovely head was shattered.

She gave a wild cry and rushed at Edgar, but he was gone, leaping down the back steps and around the corner of the kitchen. His taunting laughter trailed after him.

Gail appeared, the floor shaking beneath her tread. "What is it, child, what is it?"

"That old Edgar," she moaned, "he broke my doll."

"Oh, dear me, that boy is such a tease."

"He's a devil!"

"You mustn't say things like that, dear. Edgar," she called, "Edgar, where are you?"

But Edgar was gone. When it pleased him to do so, he was an artist at disappearing.

7

Laurel stared at the broken doll, her hands twisting at her dress. She wanted to run after Edgar, to pound and scratch him. But bitter experience told her that this would be useless. He was older and stronger; she was no match for him. Her revenge would have to be carefully planned. It must surprise him.

Gently Gan smoothed the braids that were crossed over Laurel's head and tied with ribbons on each side. "Don't fight with Edgar," Gan said. "I'll talk to him."

"I hate him," Laurel cried, "I wish he didn't live here!"

"Don't say such things, dear. You know he has no mother." She sighed.

"That's no excuse," Laurel countered. She knew that Edgar was a weight on Gan's heart. The child of Gan's younger sister, Flora, he had run away from home when his father remarried. He had come here to Gan, and Papa and Mother had welcomed him into the household just as they had welcomed Gan herself. Of course she understood all that, but it did not alter the fact that she and Edgar feuded most of the time, openly or secretly. Occasionally they had strange unnatural truces, and teamed up for some purpose, usually Edgar's. But now that he had destroyed Mary, she could not imagine ever making peace with him again.

She took from the cupboard a long-cherished Huyler's candy box with red roses on it and went out to the fatal rock. Getting down on her knees, she carefully picked up the pieces and placed them in the box.

Finally, when the remains of the doll were all in the box, she put the top on quickly, resolving to remember Mary only as she had been. Holding the box tenderly, she went to the woodshed and got a hilling hoe. Then she crossed the woodpile and turned left down a winding lane bordered with aspen trees and raspberry bushes. Halfway along the lane, beside the rail fence she came to the burying ground for pets. She dug the grave, placed the box in it, and covered it over, replacing the turf on the little mount. Then she found a

white flint rock for a marker. She ran one arm over her damp
forehead, stood gazing down at the grave. Though she could
not put it into words, she felt there was something symbolic
in this burial. As with other burials, it was an end and a
beginning.

chapter

2

THE NEXT morning at breakfast, Mrs. Prickett announced shortly, "I have discharged Brindy."

Gan started. "What did you say, Mrs. Prickett?"

From her seat at Mother's place at the head of the table, Mrs. Prickett repeated her statement, adding, "I can't stand a slovenly servant. Last night when I went into the kitchen, I saw lettuce leaves floating in the dishpan."

"Probably an accident," Gan said. "Brindy has been with us for years."

"I know she has. I reckon that's why she's gotten so lax. The kitchen stove looks as if it hadn't been cleaned since Noah came out of the ark."

"Dear me," Gan answered, "can't you just talk to her and give her another chance?"

Suddenly Laurel knew the truth from hints and signs she had noticed the day before. "I'll bet she got mad and quit when you fussed with her."

Mrs. Prickett's competent nose pointed toward Laurel, her glasses glinted. "I'll thank you not to contradict me. Can you cook, young lady?"

"I should say not!" This was no time to admit that Gan had taught her how to make tea cakes and applesauce.

"Very well I'll cook myself. You can set the table and wash the dishes. Goodness knows, you are big enough to help."

"Yah, yah," Edgar chortled. "She's going to put you to work for a change."

Glancing from Mrs. Prickett's firm mouth to Edgar's darting black eyes, Laurel felt suddenly that she was surrounded by enemies. In mute defiance, she put half a buttered biscuit in her mouth.

Mrs. Prickett fixed her attention on Edgar. "I'll expect you to bring in fresh water for the kitchen and the front porch. Also, you are to keep the kitchen woodbox full of firewood."

Edgar stopped his chortling. "Doggone it, I've got other things to do."

Mrs. Prickett turned to Chris and Roy, who sat side by side on her left. "You children can pick the vegetables. There's no reason why you all should live in idleness. I always say an idle brain is the devil's workshop."

Gan's face was grave. "Mrs. Prickett, may I have a word with you after breakfast?"

"Certainly, Mrs. Bowling, any time."

Laurel pressed Gan's arm. If Gan went to bat there was still hope. The trouble was that Gan might not feel that she could overrule Mrs. Prickett. She had distinctly heard Mother telling Gan that she didn't want her to feel that she had everything on her shoulders that summer, that that was

11

why she was employing a housekeeper. Gan, she knew, was a stickler for wishes and rights.

Perhaps Uncle Walter—no, he had his mind on Jenny, he wouldn't bother about such things. At that moment the screen door of the kitchen slammed, and she heard him call out, "Here's the milk, Brindy. Brindy, where are you?"

He came on into the dining room, the sleeves of his blue shirt rolled up, his hair standing up like wheat straw. "Where's Brindy?" he asked. "That milk ought to be strained and put in the icehouse."

"I'll strain the milk," Mrs. Prickett said. "Brindy is gone."

"Gone?" He sat down at Papa's place and began to butter a biscuit.

Pouring his coffee, Mrs. Prickett explained.

He ate as he listened, and Laurel saw at once that it made no difference to him. He was an agricultural student at VPI, and all he cared about was cows and his girl. Mother had remarked that he was in love and just wasn't himself this summer. Gan had agreed.

Laurel considered him now, wondering about his love. What was love really like? There was enough about it in the books she read, but the question was still unanswered. She had accepted the fact that Love awaited her somewhere in the future. The future was like golden fuzz, alluring and impenetrable. Beyond love was marriage. She vaguely pictured herself in a veil and trailing white dress going up a long church aisle carpeted in red. That was the extent of the picture.

But the mysterious future held other things too: Travel, Europe, perhaps the Orient. All of these things were to be hers by a sort of right, the mandate of life itself. Though she asked many questions, she did not doubt the future.

Uncle Walter said, "Pass me the jam, Laurel."

She passed it, recalled suddenly to the present by the odor of the stables that clung about him. She did not mind it especially. Fresh milk, hay, and the unmistakable note of cow dung. Papa never milked, leaving the job to Brindy's husband, Booker, so the smell was new at the table. She surveyed Uncle Walter quizzically, wondering if his girl, Jenny, would be bothered by it.

"What kind of girl is Jenny?" she asked as he cushioned his buttered biscuit with blackberry jam.

He flushed clear up to the roots of his bristly sunburned hair. "She's a nice girl," he answered gruffly.

"Does she like cows?"

He frowned. "Sure. Anybody with sense likes cows."

On his right Edgar turned his head away and held his nose. He commented in a hoarse whisper, "They stink."

"Edgar!" Gan's voice rang high in outrage.

Roy nudged Chris and tittered delightedly.

Laurel, who had gone to sleep the night before plotting vengeance against Edgar, glared at him with renewed hostility. He had no right to worry Gan. He knew perfectly well that she hated words like that. If he had been younger, Gan would have promptly washed his mouth out with soap. Now she would just have to have another talk with him. She had talked to him the night before about the doll, but he had come out looking sullen. He needed a lot more talking to.

Chris, his eyes on the butterfly net in the corner, started to slide away from the table. Roy was about to follow.

"Excuse yourselves," Gan said with what for her was a degree of sharpness.

"Mrs. Bowling," Mrs. Prickett asked, "have you forgotten the dewberries?"

"Dear me, that's right, the dewberries. Chris, you and Roy have to pick two gallons of berries each before you play."

"Aw, shucks," Chris wailed.

"Excuse me, I'm going to get my bucket." Roy dashed through the kitchen door.

He was afraid, Laurel concluded, that someone would also remember the vegetables. On her own account she was thinking fast. She usually picked berries, too, but Mrs. Prickett had said she had to do dishes now that Brindy was gone. It would be cooler in the house, but that job might lead to cleaning the stove. She turned to Gan. "Excuse me, I'll go with them." She followed Roy.

"That old hen cat," he flashed, "I'd rather be out of the house anyway when she's here."

"Me, too." Grabbing a bucket, she rushed with him into the back yard, while Chris trailed them, his net in one hand, the bucket in the other. Sir Julian, the brown-and-white English pointer, bounded out to join them.

They took the red rutted plantation road that ran through wheat and tobacco fields, down a slope through pine woods, then across the Big Branch, which Laurel regarded as hers, and up a rocky hillside to the berry patch. Here, though the land was too poor to cultivate, the wild dewberries grew in profusion.

Out of sight of the house, they slowed to a walk. "What do you mean, hen cat?" she asked Roy. "There's no such thing."

Roy shrugged. "Sure, I know that, but it sounds good and mean, and Gan won't wash out your mouth for those words."

She regarded Roy thoughtfully. He was smart for ten, that was why you had to watch him. Chris, working on his butterfly and wild flower collections for the fair, you knew how to place. He divided his time pretty well between those hobbies and his pet pigeons. Roy was different. Shrewd at figuring things out, he was likely to get ahead of you.

She saw Brindy coming up the path from her cabin by the wild plum thicket and lingered behind the boys to speak to her. She began abruptly, "What made you quit, Brindy?"

Brindy, who had removed her apron and now had a basket in her hand, answered briefly, "I'm a-going to the store to trade my eggs."

"Why don't you just tell me? You don't like Mrs. Prickett, do you?"

Brindy's fathomless dark eyes gazed into the distance. "Reckon we don't see eye to eye."

14

Laurel laughed. "Same here."

"Don't get notions," Brindy said sternly. "Your Pa and Ma done left her there. You behave yourself and mind her."

"It's easy for you to talk, you can even move if you want to."

"Who said anything 'bout moving? You Pa said Booker and me could stay in that cabin long as we live."

"Then Booker didn't quit, too?"

"Trying to catch me?" Brindy grinned. "You think that man's going to leave his crops, let alone your Ma's garden? No, siree.

"When they get back this fall, will you cook for us again?"

"What you think? Your Ma's going to need me worse than ever. After all that sashaying round in fine hotels, she'll be so spoiled she can't make her own bed."

Laurel was satisfied, not so much by the words as by the affection in Brindy's tone. She cried impulsively, "I wish it were fall now!"

"Don't you be wishing your time away. Thought you loved summer."

"I do love summer, but things are so different this year with them gone."

Brindy said meditatively, "You'll be thinking 'bout boys soon. When you going to put on shoes?"

Laurel glanced down at her feet, already brown and briar-scratched. Mother had told her she ought to keep her shoes on this summer, then she'd been so busy packing and getting ready for the trip that she had apparently forgotten the matter. Laurel thought how delicious it had been to thrust her bare feet into the grass the day after school was out. It was worth wearing shoes all winter just to have that wonderful feeling when you took them off.

"Maybe I never will put on shoes for good," she said.

Brindy laughed. "That's what you say. Go on, pick your berries, honey. I got to be getting to the store."

Breaking into a gait between a skip and a lope, Laurel

15

caught up with Chris and Roy at the branch, where they were squatting down in the shallow water looking for crawfish, while Sir Julian watched from the bank. She joined them, and for a time they gazed happily at the mysteries of underwater life. There were plenty of straw minnows darting about, and shiny black tadpoles polka-dotted the pool behind the sandbar. She saw the feelers of a crawfish emerge from under a rock, followed by the body with its dainty fan tail. Papa always said a crawfish was like a miniature lobster. Chris thrust down a cupped hand in front of it; immediately it tucked in its fan tail and shot backwards. Prepared for this move, Chris was already holding his other hand behind it. The crawfish was captured and placed in a can of water with others of his clan. "They'll be good for the ducks," Chris commented.

They continued on up the hill to the berry patch. Laurel had a secret about picking berries, she never ate any until her bucket was full. Choosing some well-loaded vines, she started to work with her quart picking cup. The June sun shone hot and steady, and she was glad she had worn her old straw hat. As it was, she had to stop from time to time, pick up the hem of her pink chambray dress and wipe her face. A few bees buzzed lazily about, and a crow cawed from the lone pine tree at the top of the hill. The shining black dewberries were warm to the touch. Now and then she pricked her finger on a briar and recalled with regret the old kid gloves Gan had given her for picking berries. Red stains appeared on her hands to match the stains that soon framed the boys' lips. "If you wouldn't eat," she reminded them, "you'd finish faster."

"Who says we're eating?" Roy shot back.

She giggled. "You ought to see yourselves."

She was through first. With her bucket piled high, she put a few handfuls in her picking cup and went to sit in blissful ease beneath the pine tree, where Sir Julian soon joined her. The reward was all she had expected it would be. Added to the luxury of the shade, and the sweet warm taste of the berries, was the pleasure of watching the boys still toiling in the sun. She had warned them, she thought virtuously, and it served them right. But she did not choose to taunt them. Her mind was busy with the crawfish waiting in the tin can.

When they had all reached the branch again, she proposed catching a few more crawfish. Chris and Roy were cooperative. In the end she wangled the privilege of carrying them.

"Gee, those ducks will be tickled," Chris panted as they climbed the hill.

They were going up the kitchen steps when he tried to take the tin can from her. "Wait," she told him, "until it's cooler. The ducks are asleep now." Glancing over her shoulder, she saw that, luckily, this was true.

Inside, the stove was hopping with heat, and Mrs. Prickett, red-faced and perspiring, stood by the table washing jars. "It's about time," she greeted them. "I'm ready for those berries."

No praise, Laurel thought, noting the dashed looks of the boys.

The floor quivered gently, and Gan appeared. "Oh, my, what fine berries! You children do better all the time."

Chris smiled happily. Roy winked at him, and they headed toward the door.

"Wait," Mrs. Prickett called, "you've got to pick the vegetables. I want plenty of peas, radishes, and some onions."

In the commotion, Laurel slipped through the little kitchen, between the big kitchen and the dining room, and out to the back porch. She glanced at the closed doors of the doll cupboard, and bit her lips. At that moment, her big yellow cat, Dandelion, jumped down from a bench and came to rub against her legs.

She set down the crawfish and picked him up to bury her face in his fur. The muted rumble of his purring filled her ears. She put her finger on the white star at his throat and felt the vibration of his windpipe. A cat was a beautiful thing, she thought, in a way a perfect thing. When Dandelion had dined well and polished himself with his tongue, he was something to gaze at and marvel over. Sometimes it made her humble to look at such beauty, and, she told herself now, this beauty was all hers.

Two years before, Mrs. Cotter had given her the little yellow kitten that had seemed like an animated dandelion. She had cherished him, given him milk, kept him in a box in her room. Now that he had reached the age of magnificence, he gave all his devotion to her, following her about, taking his place in her lap, even bringing her from time to time a small rabbit as tribute. In a rush of tenderness she whispered: "I have you, I have you."

She heard a hated cackling laugh and looked up to see Edgar peering at her through the screen door of the hall. Simultaneously, Mrs. Prickett's authoritative call sounded forth: "Laurel, you Laurel, come and set the table."

She snatched up the can of crawfish, and with Dandelion still in her arms, sprang down the steps, ran around the house and into the green refuge of the tall boxwoods. It was cool in here, and there was a bench with a cache of magazines and books under the cushions. Stretching out, with her head on a pillow and the cat seated on her stomach, she pulled out an old copy of *Munsey's*.

Her pleasure was short-lived. Edgar appeared with a renewal of Mrs. Prickett's demand. After delivering his message, he asked, "What do you see in that old cat?"

A tremor of uneasiness passed through her. "Oh, he's just an old cat. The two grays are just as good."

His eyes narrowed. Fortunately, she had already put the can of crawfish under the bench, and he didn't notice that. For an instant, they stared at each other in silent hatred. When he had gone, she got up slowly, and, taking Dandelion with her, went to the house. The kitchen was steaming and fragrant with the smell of cooking berries.

"Leave that cat outside," Mrs. Prickett ordered, "and wash

your hands before you touch the dishes."

She obeyed with deliberation. Gan sitting on the kitchen porch, which was shaded by a large old locust tree, was shelling peas. Owing to her size, she liked to do sitting-down jobs, but her hands were always busy. Laurel paused to tuck up a strand of the soft white hair that strayed over Gan's high forehead. Gan smiled. "Thank you, honey."

Laurel went to the cupboard in the little kitchen and took out a stack of assorted plates that were used for everyday. The good china with the gold bands stayed in the built-in glass doored press in the dining room. That china, Mother always said, was reserved for high days and holidays. Laurel found the dining room cool and pleasant at this hour. The shades were pulled down over the two long front windows, and the table was covered with mosquito netting, on which rested two pieces of fresh flypaper. In the soapstone fireplace stood an earthen jar filled with day lilies and the fernlike, airy sprays of asparagus that had been allowed to go to seed.

Laying the table, she gave herself her favorite plate, an odd one of real china decorated with pink roses. Brindy knew that she loved it and always gave it to her. Despising herself a little for doing it, she gave Mrs. Prickett a common thick plate with a crack across it.

When the job was done, she escaped into the hall just as Edgar came in with the mail, which he had brought from the box on the big road. Ignoring her, he sat down in an armchair and began with an air of great importance to open a package. "So it's come at last," he said mysteriously.

Her curiosity getting the better of her, she stole over back of his chair. He promptly covered the contents of the package with the wrapping paper. She waited without comment. Finally he burst out, "Doggone it, I don't care whether you see it or not." He threw the paper on the floor, and she saw that he was holding a book about half an inch thick. On the jacket was the picture of a ship, above it the title: *The Sinking of the "Titanic."*

19

She remembered now the excitement last year when the news had come out in the Lynchburg paper. For days, it seemed, the family had talked of nothing else. Even she, who never read the paper, had been curious. The *Titanic*, on its maiden voyage, had struck an iceberg off the coast of Newfoundland, and gone down; 1513 people had been lost. Over five times as many people as lived in Pigeon Run, she had told herself, yet somehow she had remained dry-eyed and detached. After all, she didn't know any of those people. How could you cry over people you didn't know?

Edgar turned to the picture of an iceberg floating on the sea. It made her think of the Rock of Gibraltar painted white.

"Well, got my prospectus," Edgar announced, not particularly to her, "now I can get out and sell some books."

His air of superiority was so unbearable that she turned away and began playing an exercise on the piano.

Gan came in, and he gave her the rest of the mail, mentioning the prospectus in an offhand manner.

"If you're going out this afternoon you'll need a horse," she said. "Better tell Billy."

"That old Billy, he thinks I ride too fast. Maybe you'd better tell him. Tell him I want the colt, not old Lotus."

Gan, eagerly looking through the letters, was only half listening. She slit open an envelope with a hairpin and began reading. "Well, well, Devoe Leigh wants to come here for his honeymoon."

Laurel whirled around on the piano stool. "Here? Seems to me he'd go to New York or somewhere."

"That would be expensive, and he's just getting started in the tobacco business. It will be a long time before he's an auctioneer like your Uncle Tom."

Laurel smiled at the thought of Gan's brother, her Great-uncle Tom. He wore a rakish white goatee and talked fast, in funny little jumps, a result no doubt of his years of tobacco auctioneering in Lynchburg. Then her interest swung quickly to the honeymoon couple. "Who's the girl? Is she pretty?"

Gan read on for a while before answering, "She's a Miss Sylvia Lytel from Roanoke, and she's been visiting her aunt in Lynchburg. They'll be married quietly at the aunt's home Saturday morning and take the afternoon train to Pigeon Run. Let's see, this is Tuesday. We'll have to wash the curtains in the Company Room and wax the floor."

Edgar, who was still intent on his prospectus, suddenly cried out, "Oh, boy, all those people drowning in that ice water. Folks will sure get a view now of that. Ought to sell plenty."

Gan looked at him sternly. "I declare, Edgar, you sound as if you're glad they drowned."

"Of course I'm not glad; but if they had to drown, I might as well get something out of it." He stretched out his legs and settled back to read further.

Laurel shot him a glance. I'm going to fix you, she vowed silently, just you wait.

Gan was saying half to herself, "It's too bad about Brindy, we'll need her now."

"They'll actually be here," Laurel said dreamily, "the first night."

"What are you talking about, child?" Gan's tone was reproving.

Laurel didn't answer. She knew and didn't know what she was talking about. The novels she read usually ended with the engagement kiss and the prospect of elysian bliss stretching like a rose strewn path into the future. At the very latest they ended at the altar. Beyond the altar one did not go either in books or imagination. At least that was the voiceless tabu that she had more or less bowed to until last summer. Then Nada, the daughter of Mother's divorced friend, Jewel —called "Aunt" Jewel by courtesy—had spent a month at Blue Ridge View while her mother took a trip to Montreal. Nada, who was charming and wise, and already going with boys at fourteen, took upon herself the enlightenment of Laurel in the shadowy seclusion of the boxwoods. Laurel's first reaction had been one of fierce denial. It couldn't be true that Papa and Mother, not Papa and Mother—But Laurel herself, Nada pointed out, was tangible evidence to that fact. Laurel had not been able to hold out against this argument, but she filed the information away in a separate compartment of her mind, where she could examine it occasionally with fascinated wonder, yet not mix it up with her everyday life. Soon afterwards, when she herself was confronted with "the lunar mystery" as someone had called it, she realized that Nada's story was confirmed. Yet a reluctance to accept this new knowledge, still made her regard sex as somehow belonging to a secret and separate world.

Now, at the thought of Devoe and his bride, the soft insinuating tones of Nada came back to her, and she was filled with a strange, tingling anticipation.

The sudden clamor of the dinner bell manned by Mrs. Prickett broke up her contemplation, and she followed Gan into the dining room, where the others soon joined them. It was notable that Mrs. Prickett, despite having to get her regime under way and can the berries all in one morning, was managing to have dinner ready promptly at twelve-thirty. What Laurel noticed more, however, with a rush of silent rage was that Mrs. Prickett had switched plates, giving herself the china one with the roses, and Laurel the common one with the crack. The horrid part of it was that you couldn't say a word about it.

While she ate the fresh green peas, the creamed onions, the crisp radishes, the hot brown corn pones, and the ham that Uncle Walter carved with traditional thinness, she consoled herself with her plot against Edgar.

Late in the afternoon, before he returned from his bookselling expedition, she concealed the can of crawfish in her apron and smuggled it up to the Middle Room above the hall. Roy and Chris slept in the big double bed with the carved Victorian headboard, and the single bed under the plastered slope of the wall that created the dormer window, was Edgar's. Hurriedly she turned back the covers, removed the crawfish one by one from the can of water, and set them free between the cool white sheets. Then, with great care, she tucked the covers in again, and went downstairs bursting with satisfaction and triumph.

chapter
3

AT NINE when Gan kissed her and told her it was time for bed, Laurel went up the crooked flight of stairs to her room on the west end of the house over Papa and Mother's room. The heat of the day had been held in by the sloping plaster walls, and the room was still breathlessly hot. She lit the lamp, but she did not go to bed. Leaning out of the front window, she could not hear a sound from the Middle Room, where Roy and Chris were no doubt already asleep. Edgar, she knew, was still down in the hall going over his prospectus.

She gazed idly at the light blur of roses along the edge of the roof, and out into the softly stirring foliage of the cutleaf

24

maple. Beyond, toward the front of the yard, on both sides of the walk, were the mammoth conical shapes of the old cedars, whose age no one exactly knew. She moved on to the little west window, close beside the tall brick chimney, opened the screen, and thrust her head out into the cooler air. The boxwoods in their irregular crescent towered higher than the house, and they, too were very old. To the right of the boxwoods on the edge of the back yard stood Uncle Cam's little house. In slavery days it had been the overseer's office. There were two double beds in it, and Uncle Walter was using one of them.

She was wondering when Uncle Cam would make another one of his unheralded appearances, when a wild yell shattered the quiet of the summer night. Edgar!

Rushing to her north window, she removed the screen, climbed out on the roof of the back porch and crept softly to the window of the Middle Room. As she reached it, the lamp was lit, and she saw Edgar in his long white nightshirt dart back to his bed and haul off the covers. At sight of the crawfish he gave another yell, not of fright this time, but of anger. He turned on the other bed, where Roy and Chris were sitting up staring about like two sleepy owls. He grabbed them each by the back of the neck and was starting to bang their heads together, when Laurel intervened. "Stop it!" she cried. "They didn't do it, I did."

He whirled, glared in her direction, though she knew he could not see her in the darkness. A black flush ran under his skin from his neck to the hairline. His eyes gleamed oddly. Suddenly, remembering stories of his father's violent rages, she was afraid.

"I'll get you for this," he snarled.

Someone thumped on the door, and Uncle Walter strode in. "What's going on here?"

"That Laurel—" Edgar began.

The next morning there was a session with Gan, and she could only be thankful that it was Gan, not Mrs. Prickett.

25

They were facing each other in Gan's airy sunny bedroom that formed the wing opposite the kitchen. Gan's great hazel eyes were grave under their black brows. "Laurel, I am surprised at you, a big girl, almost a young lady."

"He broke my doll."

"Your doll—I thought you had given up playing with dolls."

"Maybe I had, but I wanted to keep them. Besides he had no right. He broke Mary." In spite of herself, her voice trembled. Gan cleared her throat. The neat white coil of hair on top of her head gleamed in the sunlight.

"That was wrong," she said, "but two wrongs do not make a right."

"I had to pay him back, I just had to. Don't you see I had to, Gan?" She wanted Gan to see, Gan had to see. She felt but could not put into words the terrible urgency of her pride.

"Paying back doesn't really help you," Gan pointed out. "Haven't you found that out before this? Now Edgar will feel he has to pay you back. It's like a chain of wickedness. Somebody has to break the chain by forgiving the other one."

"Then it's Edgar's time to forgive. We're even."

Gan was silent for a while, frowning slightly in concentration. Finally she said, "If you go just by arithmetic, my dear child, perhaps that's true. But there are other things. Edgar has inherited an unhappy disposition from his father. In his heart, he feels that this isn't really his home, that he is just tolerated here. He takes things for slights that aren't slights."

"That's silly," Laurel retorted. "Papa and Mother don't make any difference between him and the rest of us. Neither do you. He's mean, that's all."

Gan looked at her steadily. "I expect better of you than that, Laurel. If I didn't expect better of you, I wouldn't be talking to you this way. You're a big enough person to forgive Edgar." Gan smiled, and her smile was beautiful.

Under the influence of Gan's confidence, Laurel felt that

she was capable of forgiving anything of anybody. "All right," she said, "I will."

Full of high resolve, she stepped out onto the back porch, where Edgar was shining his shoes in preparation for a day of book selling. Not giving herself time to waver, she blurted, "Let's quit all that fussing and be friends, Edgar."

He glanced up with the blacking brush in one hand. Little sparks shot from his eyes. "You're scared of what I'm going to do to you."

Meeting his gaze, she knew deep inside her that she was scared, but the last thing in the world that she intended to do was to let him know it. "Why can't you be your age?" she taunted and started down the back steps.

"Laurel, you Laurel!" Mrs. Prickett bustled out from the little kitchen. Her head was tied up in a towel, and she carried a bucket of water and a mop. "Come on upstairs, we've got to get the Company Room ready."

Laurel burned with distaste and anger. "That's Brindy's work. If you hadn't turned her off—"

"Look here, Laurel Carlton, I don't want any back talk from you. Mr. Leigh and his bride are your kinfolks. Anybody'd think you'd be glad to fix for them."

Laurel thought a minute. She could just refuse point blank and see what Mrs. Prickett would do. But that would cause more trouble for Gan. Besides both Papa and Mother had told her to mind Mrs. Prickett.

"Ha! Ha!" Edgar chortled. "You've got a walking boss now, old lazy bones."

She turned on him wrathfully, but Mrs. Prickett interrupted. "See here, Edgar, 'tend to your own business. Come on, Laurel."

Her last words were not unkind. Deciding not to protest further this time, Laurel followed her up the steps that led from the hall to the Company Room and the Middle Room. The room destined for the bride and groom looked to her clean enough as it was.

"Better roll up the rugs and take them out to the back yard to shake them." Mrs. Prickett herself began removing the white organdy curtains.

Slowly Laurel started picking up the Oriental scatter rugs that were worn but still bore a look of elegance. Mother always said they went well with the solid old mahogany furniture. When she took the first armload down, Edgar wasn't on the back porch. Then she saw him galloping across the front lawn on the colt, Byron. She felt a twinge of resentment. She loved Byron and liked to ride him herself. She was not at all sure that Edgar treated him well. Edgar, always Edgar, she thought.

Upstairs again, she found that Mrs. Prickett had piled the curtains on the landing and was busy mopping the floor. She paused long enough to say, "When you take down the rest of the rugs, bring up a pan of hot water with ammonia in it, and some rags. I want you to wash the windows."

Sighing, Laurel wiped the perspiration from her upper lip with one scratched brown arm. If this was a sample of the life she had to live all summer, she wasn't at all sure she could stand it.

But the next afternoon when she and Mrs. Prickett were making up the bed with rose-scented sheets, her thoughts were centered on Devoe and Sylvia as she was calling them in her own mind. Gan of course would insist on the prefix "Cousin" when she spoke to them.

Mrs. Prickett was saying to herself, "Mr. Prickett and I went to Norfolk on our honeymoon."

Laurel glanced at her in surprise. "Did you have a good time?"

Mrs. Prickett flushed. "Certainly. We went bathing every day. I couldn't swim, but Mr. Prickett was a good swimmer, and he looked after me."

"Did you wear stockings?"

"I should say I did. And a full skirt with bloomers."

Laurel tried to picture Mrs. Prickett as a bride, and found

it difficult. But once there must have been a young Mrs.
Prickett being kissed by a young Mr. Prickett in a hotel room
in Norfolk. "Were you embarrassed," she asked, "to be alone
with him in a room for the first time?"

Mrs. Prickett's ruddy face became russet. "Really, what a
question! Here, straighten this bolster."

They put the pillows in place and stood back to survey
their handiwork. The white counterpane, which had been
crocheted by Gan, made a beautiful contrast, Laurel
thought, to the deep glow of the mahogany. The bed was
perfect. A pity it had to be touched, slept in. Sometimes she
had felt that way when looking at the table set for company
with its gold banded china, its silver, its pink roses in the
round glass vase. For a moment perfection seemed actually
achieved, then, quickly and methodically, it was destroyed.
She turned about slowly eyeing the fresh white curtains, the
clean rugs, the waxed floor, the blue bowl and pitcher on the
marble-topped washstand, the fireplace with its bouquet of
asparagus fronds. "It looks so nice," she murmured, "I wish
it didn't have to be messed up." She added cheerfully, "but
it's only Thursday. It can stay nice all of Friday and most of
Saturday."

Mrs. Prickett adjusted the folds of a curtain in the front
dormer window. "What a notion. We fixed the room to be
used."

Laurel's thoughts turned again to Sylvia and Devoe. "Anyway it's better to have a bride and groom than somebody like
Aunt Cordelia. She really wrecks a room."

"Tish, tish. Come on down and set the table for supper."

Laurel followed slowly to the landing, then slid down the
bannister to the hall, alighting neatly on both bare feet.
"Laurel," Mrs. Prickett cried, "you are too big for tricks like
that. It's not ladylike."

"You don't treat me like a lady, you treat me like a child."

Ignoring that, Mrs. Prickett hurried on toward the
kitchen.

Laurel's rebellion surged up anew. What a summer she had ahead of her. Between Mrs. Prickett and Edgar, she wouldn't have a moment's peace.

Friday morning she tried to escape with Chris and Roy to the dewberry patch, only to be told by Mrs. Prickett that she had to stay and help with the baking. It did no good to protest that she knew nothing about cakes and pies except that she liked to eat them. Tied up in one of Gan's black-and-white checked aprons, she stood by the table beating eggs with a silver fork, while Gan sat on the kitchen porch creaming the butter and sugar. Mrs. Prickett rushed about firing the stove, getting pans ready, sifting flour.

Laurel thought longingly of the cool boxwoods, of the still cooler swimming hole. But even with both outside doors open, the room steamed like a cauldron. The whole operation was an offense against the June morning. But company was coming, and preparations had to be made. Neither Mrs. Prickett nor Gan would ever question a custom of such ancient standing.

Unexpectedly Laurel felt a pleasant furry touch on her legs and glanced down to see Dandelion rubbing against her. He gazed up with his big golden eyes and purred consolingly. His back was delicately arched, his tail a plume of splendor. She longed to kneel down and pet him. He at least understood.

"Scat!" Mrs. Prickett waved her apron, and pushed him toward the door with her foot.

"Don't!" Laurel cried. Before his ignominious exit could be accomplished, she snatched him up in her arms, and faced Mrs. Prickett. "You can't hurt Dandelion!"

"Nonsense. I say no cats in the house, and I mean no cats in the house."

"Then I'll go with him." She marched grandly out with Dandelion clasped to her breast.

"Laurel," Mrs. Prickett called, "come back here this minute."

Laurel did not answer. She stood in the shade of the locust tree soothing Dandelion. He had stopped purring and was squirming restlessly. He was a proud cat, and she knew his pride had been hurt.

Mrs. Prickett came out on the porch and looked down at her with narrowed eyes. "I hope that cat doesn't catch chickens. I missed one of the frying-size pullets this morning."

Laurel could feel her blood stopping in her veins. Then it rushed madly up and down from her head to her toes. She couldn't speak. She knew too well the fate of cats that caught chickens. Mustering her voice by sheer will power, she cried, "It wasn't Dandelion. It was maybe a weasel or one of the gray cats."

Mrs. Prickett planted her hands on her hips. "You know very well those gray cats stay in the stable."

"Laurel, dear," Gan said, "let Dandelion find a spot in the shade, and you come back and help us with the cakes."

Gently she placed him on the ground, gave him a few fond strokes, and returned to the kitchen, where Mrs. Prickett ordered her to wash her hands.

By dinnertime two cakes that were masterpieces rested on the old sideboard in the little kitchen. One was a superb, uniced pound cake baked in the octagonal mould. According to Mrs. Rohr's cookbook there was a pound of everything, and a dozen fresh eggs. The other was a four-layer chocolate cake, with a boiled frosting that Laurel had to admit was a credit to Mrs. Prickett's talents.

But for once Laurel did not want to sop the pan. She was conscious only of her terrible fear for Dandelion.

chapter

4

SATURDAY MORNING Mrs. Prickett became a veritable Captain Bligh. Every last inch of house and yard had to be brought up to snuff as Gan said. There was no dewberry picking. Chris and Roy were dispatched to the garden to gather vegetables. The black-and-white Holsteins continued to crop the acre of front lawn, while Uncle Walter was using the hand mower on the yard. Gan sat on the back porch cleaning the silver, and Mrs. Prickett mopped the dining room and hall. Edgar had escaped on Byron, his prospectus and order blanks in the saddle bags. He would get out of it, Laurel thought bitterly, and she doubted very much that he spent all his time making sales talks. He probably stood around gossiping for hours in the store at Forest Mill.

She herself was assigned the job of sweeping out the garden house. With a broom, a bucket of lime, and a supply of newspapers and catalogues, she followed the path to the weathered little building halfway down the north edge of the garden. There was a damson tree on each side, and a trumpet vine framed the doorway. In Lynchburg, she knew, there were real bathrooms with hot and cold running water and toilets. Once she had experienced such luxury when visiting Uncle Tom with Gan. But here in the country you didn't bother about such things.

She decided to take her time and review the jewelry section in last year's Montgomery Ward catalogue. It was fun picking out any ring you liked and visualizing it on your finger. She particularly fancied rubies and had read once in her geography that they came from Ceylon. Wearing the imaginary ring, you could then picture Ceylon, and yourself riding an elephant through the palm trees to a Buddhist temple.

Before she was half through the job Mrs. Prickett arrived to inspect her work. "Mercy, Laurel, how you do dilly-dally. Stack those papers while I sprinkle the lime."

There was no letup till dinnertime. After that Laurel escaped to the stable with a basket, saying she was going to look for hen nests.

In the far end of the long fieldstone building, she found Billy Watt busy currying the two bay mares, Juno and Lady, both offsprings of Lotus, as was Byron. She had heard Billy referred to as a character. He was dark and thin and jumpy, with a slightly hooked nose, and darting black eyes that were both sly and humorous. He was supposed to have worked around Maryland race tracks in the past, but had left this job for reasons best known to himself. For looking after the horses, with the exception of the two percherons that Booker used for ploughing, he received a small salary and the use of the cabin overlooking the ice pond. He shot Laurel a glance over his shoulder. "How you be, young lady? Hear you're getting company."

"You hear right. I've been working myself to death cleaning up."

"Well, now, ain't that too bad. Thought you was just kicking up your heels since school was out." He laughed teasingly. After running the comb again over Lady's satin rump, he added, "Sure can feel for you, Missy. Mr. Walter's been on my back. Had to wash the carriage this morning."

"I reckon it needed it."

"That's a matter of opinion."

She knew that to him the carriage was a minor thing as compared to the horses. He had long ago removed the top on some pretext or other, and he had just used the term carriage with a touch of sarcasm. Usually it was referred to as the trap because you had to turn down the front seat to enter the back, and then, in case of a runaway or other extraordinary occurrence, you were literally trapped. Without the top it was of course lighter and smarter looking, and he obviously considered it more suitable for exercising the team. He took great pride in driving the bays the five miles to Pigeon Run, and was always ready to meet the train.

In the pleasant semi-darkness of the stable, she stood scrounging her feet into the chaff on the floor and thinking how much nicer it was here than in the house with the work-crazed Mrs. Prickett. She liked the smell of grain and leather and horses, and wished that she could change jobs with Billy for the summer. She said as much.

He laughed again and turned to fire a stream of tobacco juice into an empty stall. "How 'bout that widow woman?" he wanted to know.

"She's all right, I reckon, if you don't have to stay in the same house with her."

"You sure said a mouthful there, Missy. There's a whole parcel of women you could say that about."

"Is that why you didn't get married?"

34

"That's as may be. Hear this Mr. and Mrs. Leigh that's coming just got married today. Reckon I'll have to drive slow coming home."

She almost asked why, but realized in time that it would sound childish. After all, a honeymoon couple was something special and different. Never having seen such a pair at close range, she became violently curious as to how they would act.

The late afternoon was devoted to bathing. Since the capacity of the tank on the kitchen range was limited, water was also heated in the two big canning kettles. The zinc tub was taken from the back porch into the little dressing room at the end of Gan's room. In addition to the usual washstand in there, a funnel had been installed to carry off the bath water to a barrel in the back yard.

By six-thirty Laurel was scrubbed to an unnatural luster and arrayed in her white organdy dress, complemented with her white slippers and new blue hair ribbons. As the trap came in through the big gate, she was waiting on the front porch with Gan, Mrs. Prickett, and Uncle Walter. Chris and Roy, who had been playing croquet, threw down their mallets and ran to the yard gate.

Billy circled the lawn at a smart trot and drew up with a flourish. Curious and hesitant at the same time, Laurel followed Uncle Walter down the brick walk. Devoe, who was dark and handsome enough to be the hero of a novel, sprang out and turned to his bride. Instead of helping her out by the elbow, however, he held out his arms and swung her lightly from the trap to the ground. Then, with one arm still clasped about her, he turned to meet them.

Instinctively, Laurel felt that she had never seen anyone so completely feminine as Sylvia Leigh. It was as though Eve herself were standing there in a long graceful dress of old rose silk. A little rose-clustered hat crowned her blond hair, and her eyes looked out, deep and blue, from between thick dark lashes.

"This must be Laurel," Devoe said, bending to kiss her on

35

the forehead. "Sylvia, darling, meet Aunt Celia's favorite grandchild."

Laurel was submerged in a silken embrace, permeated with the scent of lilies-of-the-valley. "Laurel," the soft voice cried, "I've heard so much about you, honey."

"Hello," Laurel answered in a muffled tone. Further words dried up in her throat. In the face of all this loveliness, she felt incredibly stolid and wooden.

When greetings and congratulations were finally over, Gan said, "Laurel, will you show them up to their room?"

Still tongue-tied, she went ahead of them up the stairs, while Billy followed with the two suitcases. Opening the door of the Company Room, she felt a surge of satisfaction that she had helped make it ready. On an impulse, she had voluntarily added the final touch of pink roses on the dresser.

"How sweet!" Sylvia cried. "Oh, Devoe, isn't this the sweetest room?" She looked away from him and blushed. Then she went to the front window, drew back the curtain, and gazed out as though she had come to study the landscape.

Billy put down the suitcases. "Any time you folks want to take a drive, just call on me."

No one answered. Devoe was watching Sylvia, who continued to stare out of the window. Winking at Laurel, Billy left the room. She, as though nailed to the floor, remained where she was.

Devoe had put his arm around Sylvia, and they were now gazing out of the window together. "A sweet, sweet old place," she murmured. "You say they call it Blue Ridge View?"

"Yes. On clear days you can see the mountains to the north." He kissed her. "Our first kiss in this room," he said. "Now we've christened it."

"Oh, Devoe, I can't believe it."

He laughed low in his throat. "You won't be saying that tomorrow."

Turning, he evidently became aware that Laurel was still

present. Opening his suitcase, he took out a five-pound box of Huyler's candy and handed it to her. "Will you take this down to Aunt Celia, dear?"

Sylvia was smiling at her. "What a beautiful name Laurel is! And you are going to be a beauty, too. Isn't she, Devoe?"

"Naturally. She has Aunt Celia's eyes."

Blushing, clutching the box in her arms, Laurel backed out of the room and descended the stairs as though in a trance.

With the exception of Mrs. Prickett, the family all waited in the hall below. Roy was spinning himself around and around on the piano stool, his tow-colored Dutch bob swinging about his ears. In the corner by the cellar door, Chris was mending his butterfly net. Gan sat in the wing chair, busy with her tatting, while Uncle Walter lounged nearby, absent-mindedly roughing up his recently combed hair. Though he refused to tell anybody how many sales of the *Titanic* book he had made, Edgar was peering into his wallet with a satisfied air.

At sight of Laurel, he taunted, "Didn't you know enough to leave 'em alone?"

Roy stopped spinning. "Gee, candy! What a whopper of a box."

Laurel gave the box to Gan. "How nice!" Gan said, admiring the lady on the cover and the bow of red ribbon. "We'll open it after supper."

Already the tantalizing smells of hot rolls and frying chicken filled the air, but for once Laurel's thoughts were not centered on the coming feast.

Sir Julian appeared at the back screen door and scratched. Chris jumped up to let him in.

"No," Gan said, "better leave him outside. Mrs. Prickett objects to having him in the house."

"I don't care," he flared. "He's always come in before."

"I know, dear, but the weather is so warm it's no hardship for him to lie on the back porch."

Evidently accepting the inevitable, Sir Julian lay down with a deep sigh. If she hadn't been so absorbed in Devoe and Sylvia, Laurel would have gone to comfort him. Gan glanced up at her. "Dear, maybe you had better help Mrs. Prickett get things on the table."

Leaving the hall with reluctance, Laurel went into the kitchen, where Mrs. Prickett was dishing up a great platter of fried chicken. Together they had set the table in the afternoon, adding another leaf, and putting on the best linen cloth and the china with the gold bands. The centerpiece of roses was flanked by candles in the tall silver candlesticks, but the leisurely summer evening still afforded daylight, and they had not been lit as yet. Besides cucumber pickle and strawberry preserves, there was a bowl of applesauce made from freshly picked June apples, and a corn pudding made from fresh early corn. A tall pitcher of iced tea and a pitcher of milk waited by Mrs. Prickett's place.

"Everything else is ready," she said. "You take up the rolls."

Laurel was conscious that Mrs. Prickett had put on her black silk dress and a white ruffled apron. As a result of standing over the stove, her face was redder than usual, and her forehead was damp beneath the neatly combed wings of gray hair. After a last look at the table, she rang the bell vigorously out of the back door as usual.

Laurel darted into the hall to see the bride come down. Sylvia was now wearing a pale green voile that seemed to bring out reddish lights in her blond hair. She still moved in a cloud of lily-of-the-valley perfume. When they were gathered around the table, Laurel sat gazing at Sylvia and Devoe, who were opposite her. They were beautiful, she thought, more romantic than the lovers in *Graustark* or *Beverly of Graustark*. She loved the way he turned to look down at her when anything was passed.

Gradually Laurel became aware that others at the table were not insensible to the special aura that surrounded those two. Apparently for lack of better words, Uncle Walter kept saying, "Have more chicken." No doubt his thoughts were on Jenny, whom he was to marry after college.

Even Edgar's black eyes were free of malice for the moment, and now and then he stole admiring glances at Sylvia, who sat on his right.

During the meal Laurel scarcely spoke. She was rapt, intoxicated with the strange feeling that overwhelmed her. Intuitively, she understood that the time was rare and special, that she was sharing through a sort of empathy something that the adult knew, and unimaginable day she would experience herself. It was the way you felt sometimes after listening to music; you didn't want to speak or move.

After supper there was music. Gan sat down at the piano and played *Ben Bolt, Annie Laurie,* and *Love's Old Sweet Song.* They all gathered around her and joined in the singing. Roy's impish treble and Chris's tuneless chanting of the words were alike drowned out by Uncle Walter's deep bass. Laurel, who didn't sing very well herself, was thankful for this. Sylvia and Devoe, standing in the back with their arms around each other, were not singing at all, they were kissing.

Finally Gan began playing *The Blue Danube* very softly, and the two started to dance as though they were the only beings in the world and the music was just for them. With the last strains of the waltz, they drifted out through the front door and vanished in the June night.

Involuntarily, Laurel gave a long shivering sigh.

Roy lifted the box of candy from the back of the square piano and handed it to Gan. "You said you'd open it after supper," he reminded her.

She nodded, swung around on the stool, and began untying the red ribbon. As the chocolates were disclosed, the boys stretched out eager hands. "Ladies first," Gan said, extending the box first to Mrs. Prickett, then to Laurel.

Uncle Walter removed his coat and leaned back on the sofa beneath the gilt mirror.

Gan said: "Now that we're all together, I'll read Margaret's letter." They all listened passively, enjoying the chocolates, as Gan read:

"Dearest Mother:
We are sailing at noon today, and I can hardly believe it. At last my dream is coming true, I am going to Europe. I hope you have reconciled yourself to my using my inheritance from Father for this purpose. He believed in education, and this trip will certainly be educational.

Oh, I have something funny to tell you. I have met all of Charlotte's party now, and they are all ladies. John almost got cold feet when he found it out. He said he'd be doing nothing all summer but holding doors and assisting us into carriages. I assured him there would be plenty of men on the ship and in the hotels. Besides he could always escape to the smoking room.

New York is simply overwhelming. I feel suffocated by all these tall buildings. And you never saw so many carriages, wagons, and automobiles. The horses here are used to the machines, and seldom shy or run away as our horses are apt to do.

I trust the children are behaving, and that Mrs. Prickett and Brindy are getting along well.

John joins me in love to each and every one.
                    Affectionately, Margaret."

"Ha, ha!" Edgar laughed. "Cousin John is in for it. If the ship goes down, he'll be the last one in the lifeboat."

"Edgar," Gan admonished, "that is certainly no subject for jokes."

"Do you think their ship will sink like the *Titanic?*" Roy questioned, a rivulet of chocolate seeping from one corner of his mouth.

"Of course not. The Lord will protect it," Gan said.

"He didn't protect the *Titanic,*" Laurel couldn't resist pointing out.

40

Gan looked at her over her glasses. "There are things we can't understand, child."

Since she could not deny that, Laurel did not pursue the matter. Tonight her interests lay elsewhere.

Mrs. Prickett, sitting erect in a straight chair, smoothed her black silk dress over her knees. "Mrs. Bowling, I hope you will explain about Brindy when you write."

Gan folded the letter and put it back in the envelope. "I had thought it might be better not to bring up that subject. It would just worry them, and I do want them to have a happy trip."

"Just as you like of course. But I am sure if Mrs. Carlton had seen those lettuce leaves floating in the dishpan, she would have done just as I did."

Edgar sniggered and nudged Laurel. "Thanks to those lettuce leaves, you'll get a little experience this summer."

Laurel struck his hand away and turned toward the front door.

Gan looked at her watch. "Mercy, it's after nine. Roy, you and Chris go right to bed."

"What about Laurel?" Chris asked.

"She will go up soon. Hurry now. And don't forget to wash your face and hands."

Softly Laurel stepped out onto the porch. A whippoorwill was singing in the woods across the road. There was something lonely and wild and sad about the voice of the whippoorwill, but she loved it. Particularly now. Dropping down on a bench, she absentmindedly pulled the petals from a full blown rose. As her eyes became used to the darkness, she made out two figures, standing very close together near one of the gates that led through the boxwoods into the garden. What were they thinking, she wondered. Were they so happy that they could never be any happier? She longed to protect them, to keep them safe in this new world of theirs.

41

chapter

5

AT BREAKFAST next morning Laurel gazed questioningly at Sylvia and Devoe, but she couldn't see any great difference. The facts of love that Nada had given her still seemed a little incomprehensible. Besides she had a feeling that mere facts in themselves were only a part of the truth, that the whole truth, if you could ever find it, took in much more. It had to do with the way people felt deep inside themselves, and how far the deep inner feelings of one person could touch and merge with those of another.

A pleasant Sunday morning sound broke through her thinking. Booker was turning the ice cream freezer on the back porch. "Ice cream!" Roy cried. "What kind is it?"

"Vanilla," said Mrs. Prickett. "I think everybody likes vanilla. I hope you do, Mrs. Leigh."

There was no response from Sylvia, who was looking at Devoe. Edgar nudged her arm. "She says do you like vanilla?"

Sylvia started and blushed. "Oh, I just love it. I—didn't realize I was Mrs. Leigh."

Devoe gave her a mock frown. "It's about time, Mrs. Leigh."

They all laughed politely. Gan offered more batter bread, and Uncle Walter began serving second helpings of fried apples.

As they were finishing, Gan said: "I've told Billy to have both the trap and the buggy hitched up by ten o'clock. That will give us plenty of time to get to church by eleven. Devoe, you and Sylvia may prefer the buggy with Lotus. Edgar will ride Byron as usual, and the rest of us will go in the trap."

"Why not let me ride Byron for a change?" Laurel asked.

"In your white dress?" Gan's tone was final.

Edgar gave her a look of triumph, and she had an impulse to throw her glass of milk at him. On an inspiration she said, "Oh, I forgot. You're our groom."

"Better not get smart with me. You've got plenty coming already."

A chill of warning shot through her. So he hadn't forgotten. Well, she hadn't expected him to forget. She eyed him coldly and said nothing.

On the drive to church, she watched enviously as he galloped past them down the hill and thundered over the covered bridge that spanned the creek. When he had disappeared, she turned to see where Devoe and Sylvia were. Old Lotus was poking along at least a hundred yards behind. They wouldn't care, Laurel thought, if Lotus stopped to graze on the way.

At last the trap drew up at the little white chapel on a hill overlooking Forest Mill, and Uncle Walter tied the team to a fence post in the shade of an oak tree. They had been in church for hours, it seemed to Laurel, when she saw Devoe and Sylvia slipping into one of the back seats.

"Don't keep turning around," Gan whispered.

She desisted, but her thoughts continued to hover about the couple in loving fascination. She had a strange feeling of ownership, and gloated over the prospect of having them at Blue Ridge View for several weeks. She began to devise schemes for being near them and doing things for them. Her first opportunity came at dinner when Uncle Walter told Sylvia about the great rock on the northeast edge of the plantation, overlooking the creek. "That rock is bigger than this house," he said. "Seems that years ago a whole flock of sheep jumped off it and were killed."

Sylvia shuddered. "Oh, how awful, the poor, poor things! How did it happen?"

"Dogs chased 'em. One sheep got scared and jumped, the rest followed." Uncle Walter's tone was almost lugubrious.

It was like him, Laurel thought, to be concerned over the sheep. He was crazy about any kind of farm animal. She doubted if even Jenny would take precedence over a sick cow.

"Oh, I'd like to see that rock," Sylvia said.

"I'll show you the way," Laurel volunteered.

Sylvia gave her an unexpectedly warm smile. "Honey, that will be just fine."

"This afternoon?"

Sylvia hesitated and looked at Devoe. He nodded. "Good idea. We'll have a nice walk." He, too, flashed Laurel a smile. "Nothing like a private guide."

Laurel exulted over her good fortune. They set out in the middle of the afternoon, accompanied by Sir Julian, who was no doubt hoping to flush some partridges or chase a rabbit. She walked ahead, not allowing herself to look around unless they became so quiet that she grew afraid she had lost them.

It was wonderful coming from the hot fields into the cool

woods. Oaks and hickories grew here, and her bare feet rustled pleasantly among the leaves that lay thick and undisturbed from year to year, except when a few loads were brought in to cover the ice in the icehouse. Now and then she came upon little shoals of thick green moss, and here she paused to stand as though on the luxury of sofa pillows. Once as she stood squishing her toes into a thick green patch, Sir Julian loped up to question her with his eyes. Most things he understood quite well, but not apparently her love for the moss. She stroked the cushiony crown of his head and explained the matter. He licked her hand, and with a flourish of his tail, darted off on another quest.

When she heard the muted roar of water gushing over stones, she turned to announce, "We're almost to Sheep Rock."

They moved zigzag among the trees, their hands clasped. It suddenly struck her that they had chosen this outing in preference to staying in the house surrounded by the family. She herself was the lesser of two evils. She felt a thrust of pain, then a queer stagnant coldness in her breast. She went on again, running and not looking back.

There was a gradual slope to the top of the great rock. She advanced to the very edge and looked down the almost perpendicular gray, lichened wall. Below lay the creek, silver and winding, here and there frothing into whipped cream over the rapids. At the foot of the rock and on each side were the glossy leaved laurel bushes, crowned now with the pink of June blossoms. They were so beautiful that she choked a little, and for a brief space her hurt was forgotten. Then she remembered. Dropping down on the rock, she recklessly flung her legs over the edge.

She heard Sylvia exclaim, "Isn't it huge! I never saw anything so huge."

They came nearer.

"Laurel!" Sylvia's voice was frantic. "Come back from the edge."

45

"You ought to know better," Devoe scolded.

It was impossible to tell them what had prompted her recklessness, so she said nothing. At a safe distance from the precipice, they drew her down between them on a log, and linked their arms about her. She was no longer alone; she was a part of them and their happiness.

Sylvia sighed. "I hate to think of those poor sheep."

Laurel mused over the leader, and the terror that must have made him jump. She pictured the woolly grayish bodies of the sheep lying broken and bleeding at the bottom of the cliff. Perhaps some of them were still able to bleat. The remote disaster filled her with a delicious sadness. It struck her that you could enjoy sadness only when it concerned something that had happened long ago or far away, preferably to something or someone that you had never known or seen. She realized now that she had felt the same way about the people on the *Titanic*. What, she wondered, would it be like to have something happen to someone close to you, or to you yourself? The idea was too disturbing to contemplate.

Looking out across the creek, she remembered a discovery Edgar had once reported. "Do you like amethysts?" she asked Sylvia.

"Amethysts? Of course. They are lovely."

"Well, Edgar said he found some once on the other side. On a ledge above the creek. But he never could find the place again."

"How intriguing! Let's look for them, Devoe."

"No bridge here, but I can carry you across. You, too, Laurel."

"Oh, I can wade, I'm barefooted."

"No, young lady, you might step in a deep hole and get your dress wet. Then I'd have to answer to Aunt Celia."

They made their way down to the water's edge, where Devoe removed his shoes and socks and rolled up his pants. He swung Sylvia into his arms and started out, feeling his way with great care. Sylvia, her arms fastened around his

46

neck, gave out little squeaks and cries whenever he stepped on a loose stone.

Watching them, Laurel was enchanted anew. His dark head bent over Sylvia's golden one, he clasped her to his breast as if nothing in the whole world could make him let her go. For the first time, Laurel wondered what it would be like to be in Sylvia's place.

Then he had put Sylvia down on the other side, and was coming back for her. He picked her up lightly and easily. She felt the firmness and strength of his arms, the powerful beating of his heart through the thin material of his white shirt. She grew conscious of the pleasant scent of bay rum that hung about him. Her heart began to beat strangely, she was confused. At the same time, she wanted to escape from his arms, and to be carried on and on forever through the lazy warmth of the afternoon.

They reached the other bank, he put her down on the sand beside Sylvia. "There, young lady, wasn't that better than wading?"

She didn't answer. As he sat down to put on his shoes, she stood immobile, puzzling over this feeling so strange and unexpected. Cousin Devoe. She had seen him off and on all her life. How could he make her feel this queer different way?

Sylvia was looking at the great rock across the stream. "Poor sheep, I think they must have been killed instantly."

Laurel followed her gaze, and for the first time in her life the rock seemed sinister.

chapter
6

ONE SULTRY afternoon Mrs. Prickett came rushing into the hall to announce that she had seen Dandelion with one of the young pullets in his mouth. "I've been suspicious of that cat," she stormed, "and now I've caught him!"

Laurel sprang to her feet. "I don't believe it."

"Where is he?" Gan asked.

"He ran off into those burdocks on the other side of the poultry yard." Mrs. Prickett turned on Laurel. "What do you mean by doubting my word?"

Laurel squeezed her fingers into the palms of her hands. It wasn't so much that she doubted Mrs. Prickett. She was terrified at what might be the truth. She protested wildly,

"He—he just couldn't!"

Edgar dug himself up from an easy chair. "Hah! Bet that old tom cat has been living on chickens for years."

Looking up from a copy of *The Country Gentleman,* Uncle Walter pronounced solemnly: "A cat that catches chickens is like a sheep-killing dog, you can't break him."

"That's right," Mrs. Prickett agreed, "there's just one thing to do."

"No!" Laurel screamed. She turned imploringly to Gan. "Oh, Gan, make them stop talking like that."

Gan's hands had quieted on her sewing, she sat very straight and grave. Laurel ran to her. "I'll look after Dandelion, I'll watch him, I'll keep him with me every minute."

Gan looked around the hall. "Very well. Let us wait and see."

Laurel glanced fearfully about. There was no relenting on any of the faces. Edgar grinned.

She turned and dashed out, allowing the screen door to slam behind her. Dandelion was not among the burdocks, but she did come upon a little pile of Rhode Island Red feathers. Kneeling there, staring at the feathers, she felt first panic, then desperation. It was a desperation unlike any she had ever known in her life. How was she going to save Dandelion? With Mrs. Prickett, with Uncle Walter, with Edgar against him, what could she do? She could not even be sure of Gan. Gan was kind and merciful, but she had her own code by which she measured everything and then acted. She had lived in the country all her life, and there was little doubt that she would uphold the law regarding cats that caught chickens. Her only hope was to find Dandelion and keep him with her. But Dandelion was not to be found. A wise cat, he was no doubt perfectly aware of his guilt and would stay away from the house for the rest of the day. Also, she concluded realistically, he was full of fresh chicken and would lie down somewhere and doze until evening.

She did not see him until after supper when she caught

49

sight of him walking daintily along the top of the fence near Uncle Cam's house. Silhouetted against the sunset, his back slightly arched, his tail high, he had never appeared more beautiful. Again he had that look of completeness, of perfection, that left her inarticulate. From his golden eyes to the tip of his yellow tail, he was flawless—like something carved out of living topaz. In all of its myriad efforts, she felt that creation now and then achieved a gem, and Dandelion was one of these gems.

He walked gracefully on to the orchard gate, leaped to the grass, and came toward her, purring happily. Either he had forgotten his sin himself, or assumed that she had forgotten it. She knelt to stroke his back, to feel it arch pliantly under her hand. In an excess of love, he rubbed his head against her hand.

Finally she gathered him up in her arms and turned toward the house. Through the arch in the lilac hedge that ran between the front and back yards, she glimpsed Sylvia and Devoe strolling hand in hand toward the boxwoods.

Still holding Dandelion, she went into the hall and sat down by Gan. It was like peace, and yet it wasn't peace. In Mother's room, across the hall from the dining room, she could hear Mrs. Prickett stepping briskly about. How could anyone be so lively at the end of a hot day in the kitchen? Although she marveled at it, she could not quite admire this energy of Mrs. Prickett's. Besides, she was vaguely resentful of the fact that Mrs. Prickett was occupying the room that belonged to Mother and Papa.

Uncle Walter glanced up from the breakfront desk where he was writing a letter. "How do you spell Schleswig?"

Gan smiled and told him. "I suppose you are thinking about Schleswig-Holstein, where Holsteins were developed."

He nodded, running one hand through his hair, which was as bristly as usual.

"Why," Gan inquired, "would you be discussing such a subject in a letter to Jenny?"

"Oh, I've got to decide what kind of dairy cattle I'm going to have. Guernseys of course give richer milk."

Gan's eyes twinkled. "I should think you'd have other things to write her just now."

"What else is there to write about?"

Laurel could not refrain from butting in. "I bet Cousin Devoe isn't all the time talking to Cousin Sylvia about the tobacco warehouse."

"What do you know about such things?" His eyes fell to Dandelion. "That the chicken thief?"

She didn't answer.

"Uh-huh," he muttered significantly and turned back to his letter.

It was almost dark now, but she could still hear Chris and Roy calling to each other out on the croquet ground. They must have tied white rags on the wickets as they sometimes did when they played late. She was not tempted to join them. That would mean leaving Dandelion. Although Edgar had gone to see Mr. Miles after supper and she didn't have to worry about him at the moment, two of the enemies were in the house.

At bedtime she went up to her room, carrying Dandelion like a rich golden fur piece across her chest. At first he prowled restlessly about, jumping up on the window ledges and mewing loudly. But finally, when she spread an old sweater for him at the foot of her bed, he settled down.

The next morning she was awakened early by mewing close to her ear. He had leaped up beside her on the bed and was begging her to take him out.

Dressing sleepily, she allowed him to follow her downstairs and out into the dewy coolness of the front yard. She hadn't been up so early for a long time. The dew on the grass looked like freshly sprinkled silver. New buds had opened on the rose bushes. The ridged-up turf beneath the maple tree betrayed the zigzag course of a mole. In the stable one of the cows lowed; then came a whinny from Byron, the colt.

51

Meanwhile, Dandelion was making use of the loose earth in the canna bed. Having finished, he deftly scooped soil over the evidence with one white-tipped paw, and started across the yard at a smart trot. She opened the garden gate for him, and together they went through the boxwoods and into the tomato patch, where some of the tomatoes were beginning to turn red. They rested on a mulching of clean straw.

But Dandelion was not interested in the tomatoes. He trotted on through the rows of English peas to the broad grassy walk that bisected the garden, running from one of the boxwood portals to the fence at the other end. At the midway point was the grape arbor, the vines decorated now with clusters of green grapes that looked like jade in the morning sun. Neither was this Dandelion's objective. He continued on, mincing and winding, pausing now and then to sniff importantly at a tuft of grass and to nibble an occasional blade.

They had nearly reached the fence at the end when she realized what he had in mind. He fully intended to to escape through the paling fence into the wheat field beyond, where he no doubt wished to search for field mice or young rabbits. She seized him just in time. There was no purring now. He pushed vigorously against her chest with his paws and switched his tail. She tried to explain, but his golden eyes stared back at her with aloof disapproval. It was an agonizing preview of the difficulties that lay ahead.

When she returned to the house Mrs. Prickett was calling her to set the table for breakfast. "Put that dirty cat outside," she ordered, "and wash your hands."

Laurel clasped Dandelion tighter. The one thing she couldn't do was turn him out. He must have felt the violent thumping of her heart. He mewed and squirmed. At last she thought of the saddle closet at one end of the back porch. Edgar kept Byron's saddle in the cutting room at the stable, so no one was likely to open the door. Temporarily he would be safe there.

After breakfast dewberries had to be picked, and once more she was faced with a dilemma. If she took him with her, he would be certain to escape into the woods. To tie a string around his neck and lead him like a dog on a leash would never do. She ended by putting him upstairs in her room and carefully closing the door.

When she came home at noon, she went immediately to see how he was. But there was no answering mew, no sudden thump as he jumped from the bed to the floor. Calling "Kitty, Kitty," she searched the room in vain. Then she saw that the screen on the back window had been pushed aside. Her heart contracted into a cold knot of fear, seemed to drop into a bottomless pit. He was gone.

During the long hot afternoon she hunted for him, not even taking time off to go swimming in the branch with Chris and Roy. But Dandelion, who evidently felt that his dignity had been outraged, could not be located. That night he did not even show up for supper.

It was the next morning that Mrs. Prickett reported another pullet missing. Then she discovered a fresh pile of feathers among the burdocks and took pains to show them to both Gan and Uncle Walter.

Trailing miserably along, Laurel repeated what she had heard Papa say on various occasions about the unreliability of circumstantial evidence. But in her heart she felt that Dandelion was guilty. At the same time, she considered his guilt a very minor thing compared to her love for him. The trouble was that they didn't care. Even Gan had gone only so far as to agree that he was a nice cat.

As they returned to the house, little was said, but she caught a significant exchange of glances between Mrs. Prickett and Uncle Walter. It chilled her with fresh dread. Yet she could not argue with a glance, a look. She dropped down on the back porch, clasped her arms about her knees. It was a time to count the scratches on her legs and look for splinters in her feet. But even when she discovered a locust thorn, she did not have the heart to go into Gan's room and get a needle to pick it out.

At dinner her melancholy was so profound that finally Sylvia and Devoe became aware of it. Sylvia asked sweetly, "What's the matter, honey? You haven't said a word."

Edgar laughed. "Haven't you heard? It's cat trouble. She thinks the sun rises and sets in that old chicken-snatching yellow cat."

"The pretty yellow cat? What a shame!" Her blue eyes were solicitous. She turned to Devoe. "Let's take Laurel with us to see the mill. Maybe Billy will drive us in the trap."

"Fine. Would you like that, Laurel?"

Laurel was rising with an effort from the depths of her distress. Particularly now, their kindness touched her. Even though she hadn't been able to lead them to the amethysts on Sunday, here they were taking up for her in the midst of her enemies. Her thoughts returned to Dandelion. At the earliest, she couldn't hope for him to put in an appearance until suppertime. "Yes, thank you," she answered, "I'd like to go."

She sat in front with Billy while Sylvia and Devoe occupied the back seat of the trap. Once she glanced around to see Sylvia actually ensconced in Devoe's lap. The blood rushed to her face, and she recalled the way it had felt to be carried across the creek by Devoe.

Billy nudged her with his elbow and winked. "Leave 'em be," he whispered.

She made herself look ahead then as they went down the familiar red hill and across the covered bridge, the approaches to which were shaded by arching birch trees. Along with the clip-clop of the horses' hooves she could hear the water surging and churning over the rocks below. She loved the cliff on the other side, where a rocky shelf that Papa called his flower garden had blossomed forth in the spring with arbutus and columbine and hepatica. Half a mile from the church they turned left down into the village of Forest Mill, which, besides the mill, had a few scattered houses, a blacksmith's shop and the store.

As they passed the latter, Billy called out to the men lolling on the porch, "Hi, Ed. Howdy, Zeke."

They waved lackadaisically, their attention going to the passengers in the back seat. Laurel knew that Billy would like nothing better than to join the loafers, and this he shortly managed to do. When she had gotten out with Sylvia and Devoe at the mill, he said casually, "Folks, I got a little buying to 'tend to. Mind if I come back in an hour?"

They didn't mind. They stood gazing dreamily up at the old fieldstone mill, its walls embroidered with moss and lichens.

"How picturesque!" Sylvia locked both hands around Devoe's arm.

Laurel stood a little behind them, trying to look at the mill with Sylvia's eyes. She had seen it so many times that she didn't really know whether it was picturesque or not. Perhaps because of the coolness, it always gave her a pleasant feeling to be here in summer. Woods covered the hill beyond the road, willows and birches grew along the millpond, and more woods rose on the opposite bank.

The water wasn't running over the dam, so she knew Mr. Chilson must be grinding. They stepped inside the mill door; the whole building was filled with a mysterious vibration. It seemed alive, she thought, as alive as any person. Mr. Chilson, who was busy pouring a sack of corn into a hopper, nodded to them and called out above the roar of the machinery, "Come on in, make yourselves at home." He, like everything else in sight, was covered over with a delicate sifting of white. It was as though a restrained snow had fallen inside the mill and left all touched with mystery.

"Let's go outside," Sylvia cried, "until he's through what he's doing."

In the open again, they walked up past the millrace to the pond, where the water lay still and dark under the trees. Although she could swim, Laurel could imagine nothing worse than falling into that water. Shuddering, she pictured herself going down, down among the roots and snags into the smothering mud and slime that lay below.

Sylvia clung to Devoe's arm. "It scares me. Let's go and look at the dam."

In silent agreement, Laurel followed. To be with lovers was almost like being alone. So often they seemed entirely unconscious of her presence. They turned down the rocky road that led to the ford, then strolled into the little grove below the mill. Suddenly Devoe seized Sylvia in his arms and kissed her. He kissed her so long that Laurel grew a little frightened; it was as though he had forgotten how to stop and would go on kissing her forever. It gave Laurel a strange tingling sensation.

At last they stopped for breath, and Sylvia glanced back at her. "Don't mind us, honey." She giggled. "When you go on a honeymoon of your own, you'll understand."

I understand now, she almost answered.

They walked on then to the edge of the water and paused on a pebbled sand bar. Only a little water trickled over the stone dam. Some of the rocks were almost black, some filmed with bright green moss. Below on the other side lay great gray boulders. Perched on one of them, a little boy was fishing.

Leaving Sylvia and Devoe to watch the mill wheel turn, Laurel stepped into the shallow water and waded down toward the ford. She loved the feel of the water, the way the sand seemed to wriggle and dissolve between her toes. A team of mules hitched to a wagon clattered down the road and into the stream, where the driver allowed them to pause and drink. She watched as their white noses moved sniffingly over the surface, seeming to draw up the water by magic. The driver, Old Man Hall, tipped his big straw hat. "Howdy, Miss Laurel."

For a moment she was too startled to answer. He had called her "Miss." She glanced down at her bare legs, and lowered her skirt, which she had pulled up above her knees. "Howdy, Mr. Hall, how are your folks?"

"Tolable, thank you, pretty tolable." He slapped the lines on the mules' backs, and the wagon rumbled and sloshed across to the far bank, where the traces grew taut as the team scrambled upward.

She stood watching the wagon disappear into the woods. Old Man Hall had called her "Miss." She was still savoring this greeting when Billy came back to drive them home. He had bought a bag of peppermint and horehound stick candy, which he passed around. Laurel took a stick of peppermint and sat back to suck it in meditative silence.

It was only when a black-and-white cat ran across the road that her anxiety for Dandelion welled up afresh. As they drove through the big gate there was the sound of a shot, but she paid no attention to it. Almost any time a tenant might take a notion to get a rabbit or a squirrel. She heard Byron whinny, then Lotus.

"Reckon they haven't been fed," Billy commented. His comment implied that both Uncle Walter and Edgar were on the premises and that either one of them could have done the feeding. If he was mad, she thought, he would probably take it out playing his fiddle that night. When the wind was right, you could sometimes hear the strains of *Pop Goes the Weasel* or *Turkey in The Straw* drifting up from the cabin beyond the ice pond.

The table was already set for supper, and Mrs. Prickett did not scold her for being late. She merely asked her to cut the bread. Laurel could not remember that Mrs. Prickett had set the table before, and it gave her a vague uneasiness.

When Chris brought the ice from the icehouse for the tea he asked, "Have you seen Dandelion?"

"Not yet. Guess he'll be back soon." She tried to overlook the doubt in his eyes. Still it increased her uneasiness. Though the pigeons were his favorite pets, Chris had an understanding and love for all animals. Sometimes she

57

thought his feeling for them was uncanny. "You'll see," she said a little louder than necessary, "he'll be back by the time we finish supper."

Trying to believe her own words, she sat down with the others. Uncle Walter asked her a second time to have ham when there was still some on her plate. And Edgar appeared to regard her with curiosity rather than malice. Beside her, Gan was unusually quiet, and once she caught a look of concern in Gan's eyes.

Before washing the dishes, she put a saucer of milk and a plate of ham scraps on the back porch. Sir Julian had already emptied his pan and gone around to take his place at the back hall door. Gan seated herself at the other end of the kitchen table to wipe dishes for her, and began talking about Europe, and Papa and Mother's trip. Then, unexpectedly, she paused and announced, "I got a letter from Edgar's brother Rome today. He wants to get away from New York and do some painting in the country."

"Is he anything like Edgar?"

"You don't remember him? I reckon you were just a little thing when he was here last." She went on meditatively, "Well, Rome has lived in New York and abroad for a long time. He's different from the rest of the family."

"It's lucky he's different from Edgar."

"Now, Laurel. You must remember that seventeen is an awkward age for a boy. Edgar hasn't gotten his bearings yet."

"Has Rome?"

Gan wiped a spoon thoughtfully. "Rome is a grown man. People say he has the looks of the family."

A reluctance in Gan's tone suggested that she thought a good deal more than she was saying. Laurel's curiosity was momentarily aroused. "Do you like him?"

"What a question, child. He's my own nephew."

As she sometimes enjoyed doing, Laurel was tempted to prod her further. It was fun prodding Gan because she would never tell a falsehood as she said, and at the same time she always refused to say anything bad about anybody. Thus she was forced to transparent evasions or outright silence. But Laurel could not concentrate on heckling tonight. She was too much absorbed in her worry over Dandelion.

As soon as the dishes were done, she ran to the kitchen porch. Neither the milk nor the meat had been touched. The air was not filled with the gentle roar of purring. No furry body hurtled forward to rub itself ecstatically against her legs.

Once more she patiently made the rounds of the yard, the garden, even the orchard and the stable. At the stable the two gray cats, who were a little wild, watched her warily from a distance and kept their own counsel. If they knew and could talk, they wouldn't tell me, she thought. There was a conspiracy among cats not to let people know too much.

At last the long summer twilight drew to a close, and she returned to the kitchen porch with the faint persistent hope that the darkness would be made beautiful by the soft lapping of milk. The plate and the saucer were still untouched. Despairingly, she dropped down on the steps to wait. The locust trees were alive with jar flies tonight, and occasionally there was a flash of heat lightning across the sky. She could hear the rise and fall of conversation in the hall, and now and then Sylvia's high heady little laugh. The laugh sent a strange shiver of discomfort along her spine. It was like a premonition that she did not wish to heed.

Then the night and her immediate fears took over. She thought only of Dandelion. It seemed hours later that she heard Gan calling, "Laurel, oh, Laurel, it's bedtime."

For once she did not answer Gan. Finally she felt the floor quivering; Gan appeared at the kitchen door with a lamp in her hand. "Laurel, what are you doing out here?"

"I'm waiting for Dandelion."

Gan stood there in silence. There was infinite compassion in her gaze, and before she spoke Laurel knew.

"It's no use to wait, dear."

59

chapter
7

IT WAS a night of grief. It was as though her whole body dissolved along with her tears, and there was nothing left of Laurel Carlton at all. She lay spent and limp on her bed, and from this inanimate body something seemed to rise and float through the window out into the night and into the infinite. It was like a suspension between life and death.

At last she heard the groaning and creaking of the stairs. There was a knock, and Gan came in carrying a lamp. Setting the lamp on the bureau, she turned and seated herself on the edge of the bed. Even at this hour, her white hair was neat, and she wore a lavender shawl over her long white nightgown. She laid her hand on Laurel's forehead. "Stop crying, child, it's no use to cry over a thing that's done."

Laurel tried to find her voice, but she had cried for so long that at first she could only hiccough. At last she managed, "They killed him, they killed him."

"They felt they had to," Gan said. "Those nice fryers were disappearing one by one. What else could they do?"

Laurel sat up. "They could let him live, he had a right to live."

"As long as he behaved himself, yes."

"But he wasn't doing anything worse than we do. We eat the chickens, don t we?

Gan was silent for a moment, her forehead deeply creased. "Yes, child, we do, but we raised them; the chickens belonged to us, not to Dandelion. It wasn't as if he were starving; we always fed him."

"I don't care. How could he know the difference?"

"I think he knew. Whether he did or not, the result was the same."

"Then you believe you ought to kill anything that bothers you?"

"You know very well I don't believe that." After a pause she said slowly, "I am sorry this had to happen. But you are growing up now, you have to realize that things in life often go against your wishes. You just have to make the best of them."

Laurel felt the sting of rebellion. "But this didn't have to happen. They made it happen. Who killed Dandelion, Gan? Who killed him?" She clenched her fists. There was just one thing she wanted now, to find out who had done it. The red throb of murder itself beat through her veins. She imagined herself choking the killer with her bare hands.

Gan shook her head sadly. "I don't really know, dear. They all thought it was necessary."

"I hate them."

Gan smoothed the hair back from Laurel's face. Then she got a washcloth and wiped away the tear stains. "Lie down

61

now and go to sleep."

Laurel fell back on the pillow. When Gan had kissed her and gone, she lay staring into the darkness, convinced that she could never sleep again.

Waking in the morning sunshine, she had the momentary illusion that all was as usual. Then she remembered.

At breakfast she demanded, "Who did it?"

No one answered.

Roy asked curiously, "If you find out, what'll you do?"

She said nothing. The truth was that she didn't know. But the one important thing in the world was revenge.

Devoe and Sylvia were of course innocent. Later on, in an involuntary search for comfort, she hovered near them in the hall. As they sat on the sofa glancing over *The Lynchburg News* for the day before, Devoe suddenly pointed to an item. "Heh, Rome's already in town. Reckon he'll be down here before long." He gave her a squeeze. "Honey beautiful, I'm sure glad Rome didn't come South any sooner. He might have tried to beat my time."

"Oh, that Rome I hear so much about. What's so remarkable about him?"

Devoe wrinkled his forehead. "He's good-looking, has smooth ways. But I don't think that's it. I think basically he doesn't give a damn. That makes him a challenge to the ladies."

"Not to me," Sylvia said staunchly, "not if I'd seen you first."

Feeling left out, Laurel tiptoed toward the back door. She found Sir Julian stretched out on the back porch. He lifted his head to look at her questioningly, and tapped his tail in greeting. It almost seemed that he understood how she felt about Dandelion.

Did he realize she was not the lucky girl she had always thought herself to be? She recalled bitterly Uncle Cam's laughing remark about the seven silver spoons she had received when she was born. "Most folks think it's lucky if you are born with one silver spoon in your mouth. But you were born with seven. I call that a mouthful of spoons." He slapped his leg and twirled his goatee.

This image of Uncle Cam did nothing to help her. During the next few days, nothing seemed to help. One sultry afternoon Mrs. Prickett sent her upstairs to clean up Devoe and Sylvia's room, and from sheer despondency she fell asleep on the unmade bed.

She was aroused by Sylvia's half-whispered exclamation, "Sh-sh, she's asleep."

Devoe tripped over the ottoman and muttered.

Slowly Laurel climbed up from the pleasant abyss of nothingness. A long melodious peal of thunder rolled through the room and echoed in the distance against the far walls of heaven. Laurel sat up. She loved thunderstorms; they both awed and enchanted her.

Sylvia gave a little scream and threw herself into Devoe's arms. He held her there, her face buried against his shoulder, and over her bright hair he and Laurel exchanged a tiny discreet smile. It was like a woman to be frightened, Laurel thought, or at least it was like the theory of women that people held. Personally, she prided herself on not being afraid of things or anyway pretending not to be afraid. Once when they had all gone over to Staunton River on a picnic she had swum too far out into the swift current and had to be rescued by Papa. Then there had been the time when, in order to prove that girls were not afraid of mice, she had caught a mouse by the tail. Trembling a little with inner revulsion, she had carried it into the hall. At her moment of triumph, it whirled around and bit her finger.

Now, watching Sylvia, she felt a vague contempt, touched with something else. In her conscious mind, she did not call it envy, but subconsciously she knew very well what it was.

The room was filled with a strange premonitory dusk. There was a flash of lightning, followed by another roll of thunder. Doors slammed. There were hurried footsteps on

63

the stairs. As someone closed the windows in the boys' room across the passage, a screen crashed. There was a knock on the door. "Mrs. Leigh, are your windows shut?" It was Mrs. Prickett's voice.

"Thanks," Devoe called, "we'll look after them."

There was a moment's pause. "Is Laurel with you?"

"Yes, M'am, she's here," Devoe answered.

"Laurel," she demanded, "have you cleaned that room? It's time to set the table."

"She's not quite through," he replied quickly. "She'll be down in a few minutes."

Laurel could literally hear the pause, then the reluctant retreat. She looked gratefully at Devoe. "I—I didn't mean to go to sleep."

Devoe shook Sylvia gently. "Honey love, Laurel's in a fix. What do you say we pitch in and help her?"

"I'm scared," she said faintly.

"You won't be if you're busy. Help her make the bed while I sweep the floor."

As the rain beat on the roof, Laurel found that it was fun doing the room with them.

When she went down to the dining room a little later, she was thinking how lucky Sylvia was to have Devoe for a husband. Not only was he nice and strong, but he knew what to do in a pinch.

As she was washing her hands in the kitchen, Edgar rushed in dripping wet. His white shirt looked like white tissue paper against his chest, his hair appeared to be painted on his forehead. She laughed delightedly. "Drowned rat, drowned rat!"

He glared sullenly, kicked off his shoes, and put his prospectus to dry on the top of the warming chamber.

Mrs. Prickett turned from slicing a loaf of bread. "Why on earth didn't you go into somebody's house, Edgar?"

"Didn't have time. I was trying to get back."

"Fiddlesticks. The storm gave plenty of warning. Any sales today?"

64

"Sure. Old Man Willis."

"Better leave your clothes in the little kitchen. You can wear that old coat upstairs."

Without waiting to be told, Laurel stepped out to the back porch to allow him time to change. Roy and Chris were racing from one end to the other, shrieking and trying to push each other down the steps into the rain. Presently Edgar stalked out barefooted and wearing an old coat of Gan's.

"What you dressed up in that thing for?" cried Roy.

Laurel laughed again. "He thinks it's becoming."

Without a word Edgar stamped into the hall and up the stairs to his room. Even if it was only by the rain, it was good to see him squelched for once.

All night the rain fell. For a while Laurel lay awake and listened to it beating on the roof and rushing down the gutter. It wasn't so good for the ripening wheat, Gan said, but it was wonderful for the garden and the other crops. Laurel thought of the rain in itself. She loved the myriad silvery voices. She wondered dreamily if the voices really said something, provided one could understand the language. She concluded that it was better to feel what they said than to know—the feeling was so very pleasant.

The following morning the sun blazed down, and the earth steamed like a pudding. Soon after breakfast she escaped into the yard. Fallen locust branches lay everywhere. She chortled with satisfaction when Uncle Walter enlisted Edgar to help clear them away. Edgar never did anything he could get out of unless it was something that he particularly fancied, or something like selling the *Titanic* books that directly benefited him.

Involuntarily she looked toward the fence where she had last seen Dandelion, and her throat tightened. How beautiful he would have been this morning with the sun shining on his yellow fur. He would have jumped down and strutted before her, his tail waving, high and majestic. She ran from her grief to the other end of the yard, past the well house and over the stile into the lane, which led to the rock stable.

The lane was heavy with red mud, and here and there in old ruts the water stood in warm reddish pools. Her bare feet plunged happily into this familiar element. Pulling her blue-and-white striped chambray dress above her knees, she gave herself up to the delight of it, thrusting her feet deep into the mud and pulling them up with a low gurgling sucking sound. In the back of her mind she could hear Gan saying, "Laurel, aren't you ashamed of yourself, a big girl like you?" This vagrant thought served only to enhance her enjoyment. She did not even wonder, as she sometimes did, why a touch of naughtiness could make a thing even more delicious.

In the stretch near the stable she came to the deepest mudhole of all. As she sank in almost to her knees, she squealed. Taking a step here was really fun. You had to lift your leg high, allowing the mud and water to cascade down in a red sheet. Then you could souse your foot in again and repeat the process.

For once she seemed alone with the world, and the world was hers. Just me, she thought, and this wonderful lovely mudhole. I wish I could stay here forever and' ever and ever. She was walking up and down, her eyes on the pleasant loblolly, when someone spoke. "Hello, there." The voice was deep and lazy and musical. No voice she knew. She turned.

He was standing on the lawn with his arms casually folded on top of the white board fence. He was dark and smiling, and all in white with a violet-colored bow tie. She had never seen anybody like him. "You seem to be having a marvelous time," he said. "If it weren't so much trouble, I'd join you."

Her face grew hot, she released her dress so that it just touched her knees.

"Ah, the nymph grows self-conscious. I suppose you are Laurel?"

"Yes."

"Well, there's no mystery about me either. I'm Rome."

66

"Edgar's brother?" Was it possible that a man like this could be related to the pestiferous Edgar?

"That's what they tell me. How is my baby brother by the way?"

"The way he always is."

"Which, according to your tone, could stand improvement."

She didn't answer.

"Well, what about Aunt Celia? The same saint and queen?"

She had started to bridle when she realized that he meant just what he said. "Gan's tolable, but she doesn't like the heat."

"The heat," he said, "that's why I caught the early train out to Pigeon Run."

"You didn't write so we could meet you."

"Oh, I wrote Aunt Celia. Not the exact date. I hate to be pinned down. Got a ride as far as Cool Hill so I just had a couple of miles to walk."

She found his casual approach intriguing. "I'll take you to the house," she offered, and stepped up on the grassy edge of the lane. Then she noticed that her legs were red with mud.

"Something tells me," he remarked, "that Aunt Celia won't welcome you in that shape."

But it was Rome himself she was thinking of. She felt ridiculous standing before him like that—Rome in his Palm Beach suit and violet bow tie. She turned toward the well used for stock.

"Good idea." He swung lightly over the fence and met her at the watering trough. Taking down the gourd that hung on the well-house, he began dipping up water from the trough and pouring it over her legs.

Her feelings were a strange mixture of embarrassment and gratitude. She wished intensely she had known he was coming so she could have met him in the hall wearing her best white organdy and her blue Sunday sash. As it was, her legs

67

emerged from the sluicing brown and briar-scratched. For the first time in her life she felt undressed without shoes and stockings.

"Thanks," she mumbled, not looking at him. "Let's go to the house."

They found Gan in the hall sewing. "Rome," she said, and rose, dropping her thimble.

Rome kissed her affectionately on the cheek, and retrieved the thimble.

Laurel had the feeling that Gan was of two minds about him. As her nephew, he was welcome, but as a handsome New York bachelor he was to be taken with reservations.

After a while he said, "Left my luggage at Pigeon Run. Lend me the auto this afternoon, and I'll run over and pick it up."

"Auto!" Gan exclaimed. "Thank goodness, we don't have one. The doctor and the real-estate auctioneer are the only people in this neighborhood with automobiles. I don't like them. They smell bad, and they scare the horses."

He laughed gaily. "Well, you wouldn't like New York these days. But I see your point. I'm inclined to agree that horses look better in a country lane. Then I'll borrow the buggy. Maybe Laurel can go with me."

"I suppose so," Gan answered.

Laurel felt a surge of excitement. To drive in the buggy with Rome! Like a young lady.

The drive was memorable. On account of the mud, it was also slow. Sitting beside Rome in the buggy, wearing her white dress and her white shoes and stockings, she had never felt so grand in her life. How important she was, speaking to everyone they met, leaving them to wonder who that handsome man was with Laurel Carlton. Every time Rome tipped his panama, her pride increased.

"You seem to know everybody," he commented once.

"Oh, I didn't know who that was. A man from over the river, I think."

"But you spoke anyway. Funny, I'd almost forgotten that was the custom in the country."

"I reckon you don't do it in New York," she said.

He laughed. "Honey, they'd lock you up if you tried it."

She considered that. "Mother and Papa are in Paris now. I reckon they can't do it there either."

Again Rome gave an indulgent laugh. "I can see international complications if they did."

"It's odd," she said, "that human beings can't speak to each other except according to rules."

He turned to look at her thoughtfully "It is right at that—you might say ridiculous."

He had spoken to her almost as if she were grown. She flushed happily and continued, "Even strange dogs pay attention to each other, they sniff carefully. Of course they might fight afterwards, but I'm sure they do it for a reason."

"The reason being that on closer examination they find themselves to be enemies? Anyhow they don't assume themselves to be enemies to begin with."

She was silent, still puzzling over the idea that people on city streets couldn't speak unless they had met before.

Halfway to Pigeon Run they passed Tyler Morgan's blacksmith shop, a weathered one-room shack under an oak tree. Tyler always pulled off his floppy black hat and waved when she galloped by on horseback. Now he had a horse's foot clasped between his knees and was busy trimming the hoof. When she called out to him, he put the foot down, pulled off his hat, and, bowing low, made a great sweeping arc with it. His teeth gleamed under his black mustache, and the sweat shone on his rich olive tinted skin. Above his leather apron his blue shirt was open to expose a vee of black hair on his massive chest. "How you, Miss Laury, how you?"

When they had driven by she told Rome, "They say when he laughs you can hear him all the way to Pigeon Run."

"So he's quite a character. Pretty light for a colored man, isn't he?"

Unthinkingly, she blurted out, "Oh, they say he's old Captain Lawton's son." Then she remembered that you weren't supposed to mention things like that, and blushed.

Rome looked at her quizzically. "What is it Aunt Celia used to say about little pitchers having big ears?"

She felt stabbed. Just as she'd been imagining herself a young lady, he had put her in her place. Without answering, she drew herself up and turned her fa e toward the woods.

For a while he seemed not to notice, and then he said softly, "I'm sorry, dear. I think I understand."

By the time they reached Pigeon Run, things seemed easier between them.

"How would you like to go to the ice-cream parlor," he asked, "before we get the baggage?"

"Oh, we haven't one here." She thought wistfully of the one Mother had taken her to in Lynchburg. It had mirrors and palms and metal chairs. A great fan revolved overhead, and the long glass showcase displayed pyramids of chocolates and mints and almond balls. The smell, too, was wonderful. It was made up of vanilla and chocolate, spiced with peppermint and cinnamon.

"All right, you hold the lines, and I'll see what I can get here." He had stopped in front of Odlum and Blount's, the largest of the three general stores. It had the post office now. In fact, it always had the post office. Mr. Odlum was a Republican, and Mr. Blount was a Democrat. Hence, it made no difference which party was in power. At the moment, Postmaster Blount was staunchly backing up Woodrow Wilson. Rome sprang out over the wheel and disappeared inside.

Lady pawed the ground and shook her head. A horsefly was bothering her. Besides, Laurel noticed, there were white frothings of sweat around her breeching and where the traces rubbed against her sides. Just like a city man, she thought, to have stopped in the sun. "Come up," she clucked, and drove over to the shade of a tree.

Rome came back with two bottles of orange pop and a box of fig newtons. "Best I could do," he apologized.

Laurel was delighted. Anything from the store always tasted extra special. When they had finished the refreshments and turned down toward the station, she thought suddenly of another treat that might be possible. "What time is it? If it's nearly five-eighteen, could we wait and see the train?"

"The train?" He gave her one of his quick enveloping smiles. "Oh, by all means. Won't have to wait long."

She could tell by his tone that he thought it was a childish idea. But her desire to see the train was so great that she did not try to think up excuses or subterfuges. She did, however, think of something else. "Lady doesn't like trains," she said. "After we get your things, could we bring her back and leave her under that tree?"

He laughed his familiar laugh. Even when it was directed at you, it was somehow pleasant. "My motto is never displease a lady."

They got his two suitcases, his paintbox, and his folding easel, and put them in the buggy. Lady seemed satisfied to return to the tree, where a large shallow mudhole doubtless made the atmosphere slightly cooler. Besides she had the store between her and the train, which would stop at the station a hundred yards away.

Watching the train come in, Laurel even forgot Rome. She thrilled to the first long triumphant whistle, then to the sight of the great black snout bearing down on the little station. The smoke poured upward, the whistle was repeated. She moved as near as she dared; the ground was shaking beneath her. The engine thundered past, the drivers turned more slowly. Just beyond the crossing it stopped, stood mightily puffing and panting while passengers got down from the two red coaches, and a trunk and some bales were removed from the baggage car. She was thinking how wonderful it was when she went to Lynchburg two or three times a year with Mother. There was nothing in the world so exciting as to sit

71

on the red plush seat, to feel the preliminary jolt, then the actual start of the train. As the station and Pigeon Run receded, she felt as though she were being borne by the spirit of magic itself far above and beyond all the everyday things of life. She had a remote pity for people standing in their yards or looking out of windows, the people left behind. Neither the prickle of the plush on her legs, nor the flying cinders worried her in the least. They were a part of the train, a part of the magic.

She watched the train until it had pulled out and disappeared around the curve, then she turned to Rome.

"Thanks," he said gravely, "I never enjoyed a train so much."

She saw with astonishment that he wasn't laughing at her, that he meant it. Until now she had never met anyone who seemed to understand how she felt about the train. If she had had any doubts about Rome before, they departed. He was a very special person. This conviction led her to tell him about Dandelion on the way home. He listened attentively, allowing Lady to take her time through the mud that was turning into stiff ruts. When she had finished, he took her hand and held it tight for a moment. "So they did that to you! You still don't know which one?"

"No. Edgar's the meanest, he'd have been tickled to do it. Oh, I forgot, Edgar's your brother." She glanced at him uneasily.

"Don't apologize. Brother or no brother, he must have given you a reason to feel that way."

She did not answer. There were so many reasons that she wouldn't know where to begin. She thought about the breaking of her doll, but somehow that did not seem a thing to tell Rome.

"By the way," he said, "I didn't have the pleasure of seeing my little brother at dinner. Will he be around when we get back?"

"Oh, yes, he always comes to supper."

72

When they got home, she saw the brothers meet for the first time. Edgar was going up the walk with his prospectus under his arm, when he evidently heard the buggy and turned. He came back slowly, pausing to wait at the yard gate. As usual, he had a somber look.

Rome leaped to the ground, then came around to lift her out with a flourish. She glanced quickly at Edgar to see what effect this had on him. There was a flash in his eyes that might have been either resentment or contempt.

"Edgar!" Rome cried. "How are you, fellow?" He seized Edgar's hand and shook it heartily.

"Heard you'd come," Edgar said. Over his brother's shoulder, he was eyeing Laurel. "What are you doing all dressed up on a week day?" he snapped.

chapter

8

AT BREAKFAST next morning Rome said, "I want to paint something cool looking. Any suggestions?"

"The mill," Sylvia cried. "It's the quaintest old thing."

He nodded. "Trouble is so many mills have been painted."

"You could say that about a great many things," Gan commented.

"I know," Laurel burst out. "Sheep Rock!"

"It's an amazing thing," Sylvia told him. "Laurel showed it to us not long ago."

Rome's dark eyes met Laurel's companionably. "Will you show it to me?"

"I'd love to." Realizing that she had almost shrieked her answer, she looked quickly down at her plate.

"Anything to get out of work," Edgar chided. To Rome he said with a man-to-man air, "I'll take you over."

Before he could answer, Gan said quietly, "You both may go. I'll fix you a picnic lunch."

"Can't we go?" Chris and Roy chimed in.

She shook her head. "An artist can't work when there's too much confusion."

Chris scraped his chair angrily. "Aw, shucks!"

"Why can't we if Laurel can?" Roy protested.

"No," Gan said firmly. "And remember to say *may* not *can* when you ask permission."

Mrs. Prickett turned to the boys. "You know very well you have to pick the vegetables. And I want you to see if those peaches are ripe at the foot of the orchard."

Laurel felt such a rush of happiness that she could have started singing right there at the table. To go with Rome across the fields and through the woods to that beautiful place—she couldn't think of anything better. Then she remembered that Edgar was going, too, and it was like finding a cutworm in a rosebud.

When they started out, she was entrusted with the folded easel while Rome carried the paintbox and camp chair, and Edgar the picnic basket. Edgar spoke only to Rome, whom he evidently wanted to regard him as another man. "I'm taking it easy this summer," he remarked airily. "Of course I'm knocking off a few sales on this *Titanic* book just for amusement."

"Money being no object." Rome's face was straight.

"Oh, it's all right. But I reckon it's not so important here in the country as it is in New York. You sell many pictures, Rome?"

"Some," Rome said. "I have a wealthy patron who takes one every now and then for her collection."

Immediately, Laurel conjured up a matronly dowager

with a lorgnette and diamonds, who called Rome "dear boy," and gave teas for him in her mansion on Park Avenue. That, according to the novels she read, was the type of person an art patron should be.

"Gee, that's great!" Edgar gave him an admiring glance. "Reckon that's the way you paid your fare to Paris last year."

"More or less. Mrs. Garston invited a party of friends to go over, and I was included."

Paris, Laurel mused, he's been to Paris. She looked sideways at Rome to see if some indefinable thing about Paris had rubbed off on him. She could never believe that a person could go through such a great experience and not be visibly marked by it. "What does Paris look like?" she asked.

He smiled. "From the Arc de Triomphe it looks like a great violet bowl. Beyond that, I'd say it's a state of mind rather than a city."

Not knowing quite what to say, she nodded. She considered it a good answer for an artist to make, but she had hoped for something a little more definite. That she would have to get from Mother. Papa would probably turn her off with a joke or two about the Mona Lisa or the opera.

"What about the Eiffel Tower?" Edgar inquired.

"It's there all right—unfortunately. It's about as useful as a giant-sized oil derrick with no oil."

Edgar was evidently startled into silence by this observation.

They had crossed the dewberry field now and reached the coolness of the woods. Rome paused to take out a white silk handkerchief and wipe his forehead. He did it gracefully as he did everything. Sometimes he made Laurel feel like an awkward child, sometimes like a flattered belle. As a compromise between the two, she was wearing last summer's sandals, which were a bit tight, and last summer's blue organdy. The dress had been a little short, but, the night before, with great labor, she had let out the hem, and it was now longer than Gan considered suitable for her. She had been tempted to leave off her hair ribbons, but had not dared go that far.

At the top of Sheep Rock, Rome stood looking down the perpendicular face to the creek foaming over the rocks below. Finally he said, "I'll have to cross over to that little beach and see if I can get it from there."

He made no suggestion about carrying her, and for this she was conscious of both disappointment and relief. They all took off their shoes and waded over. Edgar sloshed boldly ahead, trying to lead them through the deeper water, but she was not to be tricked in that way. If she got the bottom of the organdy wet, she would look like a mess. She noticed that Rome, too, sidestepped the deeper holes without comment.

On the pebble covered sandbar, he turned to gaze up at the great gray face of the rock. Again she waited, hoping that the design of gray lichens and tiny ferns would intrigue him.

"Quite a rock, isn't it?" said Edgar.

Rome didn't answer him directly. After a few moments he said more to himself than to them, "Not much by itself, but if I think of the sheep, make it sinister—" He took the easel from Laurel and began unfolding it.

After he had decided on his position and sat down with the canvas before him, he seemed to forget all about Edgar and her. Edgar turned to the picnic basket, which he had set down in the shade of some alders, and lifted one edge of the white napkin that covered it.

"It's not time to eat," she scolded. "Leave it alone."

"Oh, I was just looking." He picked up a pebble and sent it skimming across the water. Having repeated this operation several times, he turned to her. "Bet you're not smart enough to find those amethysts."

She couldn't hide her surprise. He was asking her to go with him. But she wasn't interested. "If you found them once," she said loftily, "you ought to be able to find them again."

He stalked off through the trees.

She found a grassy spot near the alders and curled up to

watch Rome. His white panama was tilted at an angle. He wore no coat, and his white shirt was open at the throat. Now and then he touched the brush to the canvas, but she could not see the result. In any case, the picture interested her much less than Rome himself. As she lay there watching him and listening to the music of the water rolling over the stones, she felt that she had never been happier. Realizing the perfection of the moment, she longed to keep it. Suppose you could just stop time here and now, and have what you had forever and ever.

She was awakened by a hand gently smoothing the hair back from her forehead. She gazed drowsily up into Rome's eyes, which always seemed to have laughter in their depths, and below the laughter something that she could not name.

"Sleeping," Edgar teased over Rome's shoulder, "in the broad daylight. Don't you ever call me lazy again."

"How many amethysts did you find?" she demanded. "I bet you just imagined that ledge in the first place."

"I know what I saw, and I'll find it again. Just haven't had time." Picking up the basket, he started toward the shade of a beech tree. "Come on, let's eat."

"I don't mind," Rome agreed, "knowing the sort of lunch Aunt Celia is likely to put up."

As usual, Laurel was hungry, but she took as a matter of course the ham sandwiches, the deviled eggs, the fresh radishes, the peach pickle, and the pound cake. There were pewter cups so they could drink comfortably from a nearby spring.

"I like this," Rome said, stretching out on the ground when they had finished. "Why don't I just stay here the rest of my life?"

Laurel's heart gave a big lollopping beat and sent a fresh warm tide all through her body. He felt it, too; he felt that the day was perfect. As she did, he wanted it to last forever. Had he caught her thought? It was such a marvelous idea that she could hardly bear to contemplate it.

"You'd soon get tired of it," Edgar mumbled. He sat with his arms clasped around his hunched-up knees and bit on a twig.

"No, you wouldn't," Laurel disputed. "It's wonderful." When she heard herself say it, she knew that it was.

Walking slowly home beside Rome in the late afternoon, she felt as though she were floating above the dewberry briars and above the stones and ruts in the lane. Edgar seemed remote and unimportant. He wasn't in her world anymore, and he could never know what her world was like. Actually, it was a new world with which she herself was not yet familiar.

That night Gan played waltzes on the piano in the hall, and she sat on the bottom stair step watching Devoe dance with Sylvia. They didn't talk, just moved about as though they were in a trance. Then something happened that made her throat go taut and dry. Rome touched Devoe's shoulder, and the next thing she knew he was dancing with Sylvia, holding her as Devoe had held her, only closer. He whispered something in her ear, and they both laughed.

The wonderful feeling that she had had all day was suddenly gone. Laurel knew that she was alone, entirely alone. She was neither a child nor an adult; she was nowhere and nobody. For a little while Rome had seemed to understand how she felt, he had even understood about Dandelion. Now he had forgotten her. Was it because Sylvia was grown and beautiful, or because she smelled of lily-of-the-valley? She glanced at Devoe sitting in the big chair near the front door. He, too, was watching them. Just at a glance, his face appeared blank. Then she saw his lips move and tighten. His jaw twitched; points of light flared in his eyes.

Seeking the relief of neutrality, she turned toward Uncle Walter, who lolled on the sofa reading *The Country Gentleman*. He looked like a farmer, she decided, tanned and healthy and a bit rough around the edges. He seldom wore a hat, and the summer sun had left his nose a little too red. A

79

letter he had received from Jenny that day was stuck in the pocket of his blue shirt. What, she wondered, was Jenny like? She couldn't be very romantic if she loved him—not that he wasn't all right as an uncle.

The door of Mother's room opened, and Mrs. Prickett came out wearing a lavender voile that Laurel hadn't seen before. Devoe rose, but Uncle Walter kept on reading. Mrs. Prickett plumped herself down in a straight chair and began fanning vigorously with a palm leaf fan. In some way, she was always moving. For a while, she watched the dancers, pursing her lips and cocking her head on one side. Perhaps she was worried for fear they would wear the wax off the floor.

Unexpectedly Gan stopped playing *Roses of the South,* and broke into a jig. Sylvia and Rome parted. "It's too hot for that," Sylvia cried, and went over to perch on the arm of Devoe's chair.

Rome dropped down by Uncle Walter, and Mrs. Prickett bustled off to the kitchen. The spell was broken, and Laurel was thankful for it. Glad of the shadows on the stairs, she huddled there unnoticed.

Mrs. Prickett returned carrying a tray laden with lemonade and tea cakes. Rome sprang up to pass the drinks as she poured them. He had served the others when he caught sight of Laurel and came over with a glass that had probably been intended for himself. Offering it, he smiled down at her with his warm intimate smile; she was remembered, happy.

When Gan motioned to her that it was bedtime, she went up to her room with the contradictory feelings of one wounded, then assuaged. She lay in the darkness thinking of Rome's smile, of the little bow he had made when he gave her the lemonade.

Awaking next morning, her first thought was of him. She went to the little west window by the chimney and looked across at Uncle Cam's house, which Rome was now sharing with Uncle Walter. The door was closed, and the little building had the still obscure look of a sleeping face. But not for long. Billy came loping over the yard and beat on the door. Uncle Walter appeared in his nightshirt, and Billy cried, "Your cows is out, Mr. Bowling, every dadblamed one of 'em."

It was like him, she thought, to say *your* cows. She knew he resented having cows in the stable at all. Sometimes when he got really mad he would make unflattering comparisons between the life he led here and the life he had led at Maryland race tracks. Once when she had asked why he left Maryland, his face turned dark and he mumbled, "Man's got his own ideas always got to move."

At any rate, he usually made the best of his job at Blue Ridge View, and a few minutes later she saw him riding off on Byron beside Uncle Walter, who was mounted on Juno. Her own concern was for Papa. If the cows destroyed somebody's corn crop or vegetable garden, he would have to settle for it when he got back. One of the tenants might take it out of the fourth that was coming to him in the fall.

Uncle Walter strode in late for breakfast, red-faced and tousled. He glared around the table. "Who left that gate open last night?"

Nobody said anything. Chris and Roy looked at each other uneasily, no doubt because they so often did things and then forgot them.

Buttering a biscuit, Uncle Walter said gruffly, "I checked at bedtime. The cows were in the stable lot. I'd propped the door open when I milked so they could get outside if it got too hot during the night. The gate to the road was shut then, but Billy said it was open this morning."

"Not guilty," remarked Rome. "You know I was here in the hall till I turned in."

"And Devoe was with me the whole evening," Sylvia murmured with special sweetness, laying her hand on his arm.

He didn't respond as usual, Laurel noted, and she recalled his expression the night before when Rome was dancing with

81

Sylvia. It gave her a tiny sadistic thrill to know that he was still smarting. Then she glanced across at Edgar. He sat motionless, staring into his plate. Of course. Hadn't he been out on Byron to see Mr. Bell about the *Titanic?* Pointing her finger at him, she cried, "It was you!"

Without a word, he jumped up from the table and rushed out of the dining room.

"Oh, dear," Gan sighed, "that boy takes things so hard."

"Huh," Uncle Walter muttered. "If he wasn't too old, I'd thrash him myself."

"I feel sure he's sorry."

"Sorry! What good does that do if the cows get sick? Found them in Willett's corn field. Been there long enough to be foundered."

By afternoon it developed that two of the cows were in a bad way. Uncle Walter came to the house and demanded Devoe's help in drenching them. With obvious reluctance Devoe went, leaving Sylvia sitting under the locust trees with Rome and Laurel.

When they had gone, Rome turned lazily to Sylvia. "Want to show me the boxwoods, beautiful lady?"

"I'd love to. I just love those old boxwoods."

Despite the warmth of the day, Laurel felt chilled. She sat with unseeing eyes fixed on the open novel in her lap. Were they pretending she was absorbed in it, or had they just forgotten her? Again she had that strange dead feeling inside as though some of her had fallen to the bottom of nowhere. She listened tensely to Sylvia's laughter in the boxwoods. It had a quality that made her tingle and rage at the same time. Why didn't Devoe come back? Since his arrival, she couldn't remember that he had left Sylvia's side a single time before this. Even when Rome had danced with her, he had been in the hall watching.

Suddenly the laughter ceased, and she sat there shocked at the silence. The silence was so much worse. It seemed hours before Devoe returned. He asked at once, "Where's Sylvia?"

82

Without speaking, she pointed to the boxwoods.

"You look funny. What's the matter?"

"Nothing." She knew her voice sounded thick and unnatural.

Devoe strode through the gate mantled with golden honeysuckle and disappeared in the labyrinth of the boxwoods.

She sat there, clutching her book, until Mrs. Prickett came out on the porch and called her.

She did not see them till suppertime when Devoe announced to Gan, "Aunt Celia, I think we'd better go back to Lynchburg tomorrow. I know just happens there in the warehouse."

"Well, well," Gan answered, "this is unexpected. I thought you were in no hurry."

"It seems as if all good things have to end." He said it grimly, and Laurel saw that his face was dark and strained. Beside him Sylvia sat in silence, not eating. For an instant Laurel felt a surge of relief, of satisfaction. She did not allow herself to imagine what had happened in the boxwoods. It was enough to know that it was past, that tomorrow they would be gone, that Sylvia would no longer be here to trail her lily-of-the-valley perfume around Rome. Rome. At last she dared look at him. It was a surprise to see that he looked quite calm and at ease. He caught her eye and smiled, his special smile. She felt as though she had been caressed.

chapter
9

FOR SEVERAL afternoons after Devoe and Sylvia left she managed to go with Rome to Sheep Rock. But Edgar, or else Chris and Roy, went along. They could always say they were going to look for amethysts. She no longer believed in the amethysts herself. Edgar had probably told that big lie about seeing them just to make himself important. All she herself wanted to do was curl up in her nest under the alders and watch Rome at his easel.

There were long spaces of time when he did not seem to know she was there, but in her heart she held to the belief that he did, that he never lost the consciousness of her presence. She was too humble in her adoration ever to dream that she might inspire him, but she felt that he might like a quiet approving audience. Stretched out comfortably in the shade, Sir Julian often waited with her. Sometimes she stroked his head or his silken ear. Occasionally the thought flitted through her mind that she took his devotion too much for granted. Then, glancing over at Rome, painting away obliviously in a separate world of his own, she realized for a painful instant that she probably bore the same relationship to him. He didn't mind having her around, but that was all. Having admitted this, she tried to deny it, tried to continue basking in the sultry July heat and the magic of his presence.

One day the hope was born that perhaps she did matter to him. She was lying quietly in the shade when Edgar returned from a brief expedition and said, "Come on, you lazy thing, let's go wading."

"I don't want to."

"Why not? You just aggravate Rome staring at him like that."

Rome glanced up. "On the contrary. She's a big help."

The two brothers looked at each other for a moment, and she saw a flash of animosity in Edgar's eyes. He crashed off through the woods, whistling to Sir Julian. Sir Julian lifted his head to look after him, then settled down again. Once more the sound of the stream took over the world.

On the way home Rome helped her over a fallen tree much as Devoe might have helped Sylvia. Suffused with happiness, she couldn't even find her tongue to thank him.

"What's the matter?" Edgar muttered. "Getting helpless in your old age?"

Rome said, "No sarcasm, please. Maybe you hadn't noticed it, Eddie, my boy, but Laurel is practically a young lady, and a deucedly pretty one at that."

Edgar made no reply. He concentrated on picking up a rock and taking aim at a squirrel. He missed.

Glorying in what Rome had just said, she barely noticed. Rome thought she was pretty; he considered her a young lady. Already her mind was voyaging through an endless golden summer spent with him, walking beside him, sitting nearby as he painted. There her thoughts ended in a dreamy maze. Something kept her from trying to see the summer's end, or what might lie in store.

Because the blackberries along the lane were now ripe enough to pick, she could not accompany Rome the next day. After she had brought in her quota of berries, Mrs. Prickett asked her to help wash them and then stir the jam. Through the window she watched Rome leave by himself.

The day after that he did not even suggest that anybody go with him. She became convinced that he wanted to be alone, that he did not really care to have her around. He had just been polite. She made a grim resolution. She would not let him see that she cared. Never again would she go with him anywhere. Never unless he begged her.

At the end of a week Rome invited them all into the hall one afternoon to see his picture of Sheep Rock.

Laurel gasped. The great rock that she had always thought so beautiful was a sinister dark mass, the force of evil itself hanging over the world. At its base lay a pile of dry white bones.

"But there aren't any bones there really." Chris's great blue eyes seemed to protrude from their sockets.

For a little while no one else spoke, then Gan commented, "I haven't seen Sheep Rock for years."

Edgar stared in fascination at the picture. "All you need is the devil looking out from behind a tree."

Mrs. Prickett pushed her glasses down on her nose and tried looking over them, then she pushed them back again and stood with her hands on her hips.

Rome gave a brittle laugh. "I must say my audience overwhelms me with admiration."

Uncle Walter raked his hand through his hair and shrugged. "All I know about pictures is I like them or I don't. Just hope you don't give me this one for a present."

86

Rome turned to Laurel. "Let's hear from you."

The blood beat at her temples, her tongue was frozen in her mouth. She wanted to defend Rome and his picture, she wanted terribly to do it. But she couldn't think of anything good to say. "It—it sort of scares me."

"Good," he said. "Fear is a powerful emotion." He added tightly, "When it's shown in New York this fall, I'll let you know what the critics say. You may be surprised."

"You must remember," Gan said, "that we don't know much about art."

"Oh, I understand. A picture has to be pretty. He turned and pointed to a print hanging near the dining room door. It showed the Biblical Ruth standing in a field of wheat. Her long hair fell softly over the folds of her robe, and her face bore a beatific expression. The picture had been there as long as Laurel could remember. She had not thought much about it one way or the other. "You all like that, don't you?" His tone was challenging.

"I like it," Gan said. "She has a sweet good face."

"Of course." Taking his pipe out of his pocket, Rome strolled out on the front porch with the air of one who had shown much patience with children, but whose patience was now worn out.

Laurel longed to follow him, but that she could not do. It was a matter of pride. He had seemed completely indifferent to her for the past week, and her only recourse was to seem indifferent now. Why had he called her pretty, then more or less turned his back on her? She couldn't make him out. Baffled and frustrated, she agonized over the problem. Mother always said that a nice girl never ran after a man. On the contrary, she ran the other way. "What if he doesn't follow?" she had asked, and Mother had only smiled. Perhaps there was no answer. She only knew that, unless Rome was in it, a room was empty.

During the days immediately following, Rome did nothing while she watched him anxiously from a distance. She

87

could not be sure whether he was brooding over the reception of his picture, or was merely overcome by the humid July heat. He spent a good deal of time in his room, or lounged on the benches under the locust trees. Her work went on as usual in the blackberry thicket or in the kitchen. Whenever possible, she escaped to the boxwoods with *Lorna Doone,* seeking refuge with Lorna in her strange hidden little valley. It was her secret hope that someday Rome would come to comfort her.

But her comfort came from a different direction. One day Uncle Cam returned. He was really her great-uncle, the brother of Papa's mother, and he divided his time between Blue Ridge View and the home of Papa's bachelor brother, Uncle Weaver, in the next county. Uncle Cam was bald and blue-eyed, with a little wispy white goatee, and what seemed like a permanent detachment from life, except that he loved children. He had a dusky past that involved horse racing and an adored wife who took laudanum. The story went that he would take his winnings and pour them into her lap. After a while he lost both his plantation and his wife. Laurel sometimes questioned him about those days. His face would become still, he would get a strange backward-looking expression in his eyes, and usually he would refuse to say anything. On occasion, however, he would pass from gloom to contrition, and mutter to himself, "Cam has been a bad boy."

When this happened, she felt guilty, but it whetted rather than assuaged her curiosity.

He still rode horseback, but he rarely came twice on the same mount. Since Uncle Weaver was a horse trader as well as a land dealer, there was a considerable turnover in his stable. The only horse he kept permanently was a chestnut stallion that he rode himself.

Today Laurel saw Uncle Cam ambling across the lawn on an ancient, battered-looking pacer. As he slid to the ground, she rushed forward and threw her arms around him. "You waited so long," she cried, "what made you wait so long to come back?"

"Great goodness, child." He kissed her and detached himself. "Been looking after things for Weaver." As he pulled off the saddlebags, his mount backed her ears and showed her teeth.

He stroked her neck. "All right, gal, all right. Don't you get riled." To Laurel he said, "Reckon she's spiteful because she wasn't treated right."

Side by side they walked toward his little house, while she continued to ply him with questions and squeeze his arm. Only when they pushed open the door and saw Rome sprawled on the bed with a book, did she realize that there wasn't room here now for Uncle Cam.

"Well, well," Uncle Cam said, "who's this?"

She flushed. "Rome," she told him in a muffled tone, "Edgar's brother."

"The painting fellow? Haven't seen you for ten years. How are you, my boy?" He shook hands.

Rome stood up. "Looks as if I'm in your quarters."

"Oh, that's all right, it's a double bed. Room for all. Or take the other bed if you want to."

"Walter's in that." Rome looked dubious.

Laurel fled to the house to tell Gan about the dilemma. She was panic stricken at the thought that Rome might leave. Gan settled the matter at once. "He can move to the Company Room."

At supper Laurel did not join with Chris and Roy in the usual clamor to sit by Uncle Cam. Though she would have liked to do so, she felt that now it was somehow beneath her dignity to make the demand. She watched a little sadly as Gan invited him to sit between the two boys. At once they began begging him to take them to the creek the next afternoon. "Maybe," he said, "maybe. See how I feel."

Laurel leaned forward. "Please, Uncle Cam. I want to go, too."

"Good gracious, you'd think nobody ever took you all but me."

"They don't when Papa's away," Chris told him.

89

Again, she felt a spasm of sadness. Things were so different when Papa and Mother were away. Perhaps it was because she herself was different. Covertly she glanced across at Rome. He seemed handsomer than ever. But remote. Apparently he was unconscious of her existence.

For solace, she turned to Uncle Cam. The next afternoon it seemed like old times to sit with Chris and Roy on his steps and wait for him to finish his nap. His snoring, with its monotonous rise and fall, sounded as if it might go on forever.

"If we dropped something in his mouth," Roy suggested, "it might make him stop snoring."

"What?" Chris asked.

"Salt wouldn't hurt him," Laurel remarked, realizing at the same moment that she really ought to set a good example for the boys.

Before she could restrain him, Roy had sprinted off to the kitchen. In no time at all he was back with a teaspoonful of salt, and he and Chris were cautiously opening the door and creeping into Uncle Cam's room. Laurel sat where she was, her curiosity about the experiment winning the battle over virtue.

There was a shriek, followed by coughing and spluttering. "Plague on you, plague on you!" Through the open door she saw Uncle Cam spitting vigorously into the fireplace.

Then he came out, red-faced and muttering, and stalked through the arch in the lilac hedge to one of the benches under the locust trees. Chastened, Chris and Roy followed at a distance, while she brought up the rear.

Uncle Cam glared at them. "Needn't to think I'm going to take you to the creek. Never had such a taste in my mouth. Thought my gall had busted."

Suddenly Chris cried, "If we get something to take that taste out of your mouth, will you go?"

"Nothing but a good toddy would do that."

"I know where Papa keeps his blackberry wine." Chris was dancing about in his excitement.

"Huh, blackberry wine." Uncle Cam sounded slightly mollified.

Chris was off. Laurel heard the screech of the west cellar door. When he came back, a dusty bottle was clasped in his arms. There was a gleam in Uncle Cam's eyes as he took it and wiped it on the knee of his creaseless blue trousers. "No corkscrew," he grumbled. "I'll just use my knife." He did this with remarkable skill, and took a nip from the bottle. Then he took a second one, looked about, and smacked his lips.

They all watched anxiously. Presently he indulged a third time. "Pretty good, pretty good."

"Will you go now, will you go now?" Chris and Roy chanted as they danced about, their bathing suits swinging like tails from their belts.

"Maybe so, maybe so. First I've got to put this away. Be mighty good to keep off summer colds and malaria." Slowly and deliberately, he got up and went back into his house, where he carefully closed the door.

They waited in silence, fearing he would resume his nap, but he didn't. He came out, wiping his mouth and wearing his old black hat. At last they were off to the creek.

Laurel was startled to see Rome seated in the shade of the corn-house, which was on the right hand side of the lawn opposite the rock stable. A fresh canvas rested on his easel, and he was busy mixing paint.

"What's going on here?" Uncle Cam paused to do a little jig in front of Rome.

Rome smiled. "Thought I'd immortalize the stable."

Uncle Cam turned to survey the stable as though for the first time. Involuntarily, Laurel did likewise. And, astonishingly, she saw something that she had never seen before. The stable was beautiful. It stood there, a great oblong of fieldstone with a steep shingle roof embossed here and there with lichens. Some of the stones were reddish, some white flint; the mica in them sparkled brilliantly in the summer sunshine.

91

Uncle Cam waved his hand non-committally. "Paint it if you want to, boy."

Roy tugged at his arm, and once more they were on their way.

At the bridge they turned left down a sandy trail that followed the meanderings of the creek. On either side rose the cliffs forested with oaks and beeches and hickories. They passed John's Hole, which had a rocky bottom, and continued on to the Bathing Hole, which was smaller, but had a sandy bottom that was soothing to the feet. A natural dam of silvery gray rocks extended nearly across the stream, with two pleasant interruptions for waterfalls.

Laurel slipped into her secret room among the bushes and put on her bathing suit, while the boys changed to theirs in the open on the rocks. Gan had said she would soon have to wear stockings when she went swimming, but she could not bear the thought. Her feet loved the free feeling of the water and the sand. There were times when she regretted the necessity of a bathing suit, particularly a two-piece one with a full skirt.

When she emerged, Chris and Roy were already in, kicking lustily to see who could send up the higher geysers. Uncle Cam had seated himself on the shady end of the rocks under a tree, put on his spectacles, and opened his book. She slipped on her bathing cap, ran to the first waterfall, which was just wide enough to sit down in, and slid into the pool. Once in the water, she experienced complete happiness. The water was warm and enveloping, it held her and bore her and soothed her. It was her home.

When Chris and Roy were tired of their wild kicking and went downstream to look for mussel shells on a sandbar, she decided to float. She turned over, and looked upward between the green walls of the cliffs, and faced the bland blue of the sky. This indeed was a moment of bliss.

chapter
10

THEY ALL knew that Jenny was coming because Uncle Walter had persuaded Gan to invite her. He had grown so restless and absentminded that it was obvious mere letters would not see him through the summer. Apparently no one thought of objecting except Laurel, when Gan said to her, "Dear, you won't mind if Jenny shares your room, will you? I snore, and I don't quite like to propose putting her in with Mrs. Prickett."

Laurel was silent, thinking how hard it might be to have a stranger breaking in on her dreams of Rome. But the only other arrangement that occurred to her was to have Rome move back into Uncle Cam's house. She was sure he would

93

not like that. She had heard him say how much he enjoyed the view of the mountains from the north window of the Company Room.

"I guess it will be all right," she told Gan without enthusiasm. "I hope she doesn't kick."

On the day of Jenny's arrival, Uncle Walter insisted, much to Billy's disgust, on washing the trap and currying Juno and Lady himself. Then he took buckets of hot water and the big tin tub into Uncle Cam's room, where he doubtless gave himself a going-over just as thorough. "Love," Rome remarked, "must be wonderful."

Laurel didn't much like the tone he used, but then she realized that he was just referring to Uncle Walter, and Uncle Walter was obviously all mixed up in a sea of Holsteins and love, which made him seem ridiculous. In none of the novels she read was there a lover remotely connected with cows.

Jenny came bouncing up the front walk beside Uncle Walter, wearing a white shirtwaist and dark blue skirt, and a straw hat adorned with daisies. She had a very pink-and-white complexion, crisp brown hair, greenish eyes, and a durable nose that was more flat than Grecian, Laurel decided. When Uncle Walter introduced her to Gan, she blushed and stammered a little as she put her hand in Gan's and said, "How do you do, Mrs. Bowling?"

"Jenny. I have wanted to meet you, child." Gan kissed her cheek.

There were a few pleasantries about the train trip while Uncle Walter carried her suitcase up to Laurel's room and returned. Then Laurel took her upstairs to freshen up before supper. Once there, Jenny became busy and methodical, taking out her dresses one by one, shaking them carefully and placing them on hangers in the wardrobe. Her hat she put on the top shelf without even waiting for Laurel to tell her. When she slipped off her shirtwaist and skirt, Laurel saw that her underclothes were very white and starchy. She washed up at the washstand, using plenty of soap on her face and arms. "Those old cinders," she complained, "they get on you even with the windows shut."

When she was ready to go down, Laurel conceded to herself that Jenny looked all right. Her hair had a springy, alive quality, and little curls popped out around her face. The long blue voile clung to her full bosom and fell almost to her slender ankles. As they reached the hall, Laurel had a spasm of uneasiness. She dreaded for her to meet Rome. As the two faced each other, she watched anxiously, but she could not tell much except that his eyes flicked over Jenny fast and thoroughly. He said, "I understand now why Walter has been panting."

"Panting?" Jenny repeated in a puzzled tone. "I reckon everybody pants in this weather."

Rome laughed to himself, and Laurel wondered if she were the only one to catch a certain note in that laughter.

"Rats," Uncle Walter said loudly. "What kind of fool talk is that?" He took a firm grip on her arm and seated her on the sofa beside himself.

"Walter," she murmured. On his name her voice dropped into a special low key that seemed to express a wondering and reverential love for one so grand.

After supper when Rome proposed dancing, Uncle Walter said shortly, "Jenny doesn't dance. She and I are going for a walk."

Rome lifted his brows and shrugged.

Laurel was thankful. She could not stand to see him dance with Jenny as he had danced with Sylvia. As for his dancing with her, she could not even dream of that. She had never danced much, and she would be awkward.

Gan sat reading aloud a letter of Mother's from Bavaria:

"It's the quaintest country, just like something out of a fairy tale. The farms are all in tiny patches, and they are worked by oxen and even cows. Scythes are used for har-

95

vesting the grain. And the villages, you should see the villages! Narrow winding streets that seem hardly wide enough for our carriages. All the windows have bright window boxes, and the plaster walls actually have paintings on the outside. Every cross-road has its little shrine, the Savior on the cross or the Mother Mary. Always at their feet are bunches of flowers, some of them limp and wilted, some of them fresh picked."

For the moment, the scene in the hall and even Rome passed out of Laurel's consciousness. She was in Bavaria, riding alone in a carriage drawn by two white horses. And beside her was an outrider on a great black horse with golden trappings. String music floated through the trees, and the outrider began to sing.

The spell was broken by Edgar, lolling back on the end of his spine in an easy chair. "Doesn't sound very exciting to me. I'd rather go to Spain and see the bull fights."

"Shame!" Gan exclaimed. "Bull fights are cruel."

"Dear Aunt Celia," Rome murmured, "how can you escape cruelty in this dog-eat-dog world? I might add cat eat mouse, snake eat toad, and man eat everything. It's the law of nature, isn't it?"

Gan shook her head. "There are many things we can't understand, Rome, but we do know that man was made in the image of God, and he has the power to choose the good."

Laurel listened eagerly. She loved arguments. But this was an unexpected one and involved a subject that she hadn't really thought about. She had a feeling that Rome's stand was the more logical, yet Gan's viewpoint was something beyond logic, and maybe the better of the two. At last she admitted to herself that Rome had a certain allegiance to evil. She recalled his picture of Sheep Rock. If you were thinking of the mass suicide of the sheep, that is what you would see. There were bad things in the world, and Rome recognized them. After all, wasn't he just being sensible? She

96

turned to Gan. "You do believe there's a devil, don't you, Gan?"

Gan's forehead creased into a frown. "The Bible says so, so there must be. But we must always bear in mind Christ's words, 'Get thee behind me, Satan.' "

Rome laughed. "If you're interested in my opinion, Aunt Celia, that's a dangerous position to have your enemy in."

"You are being facetious," she answered haughtily. "It doesn't become you to be facetious on a serious matter."

Unexpectedly Edgar broke in. "What about all those people who went down on the *Titanic?* were they being punished for something, or did the devil get the best of God in sinking the ship?"

"Good question, my boy." Rome was tamping tobacco into his pipe after first getting Gan's permission to smoke.

"A true believer doesn't ask such questions," Gan said. "He has faith."

"Then nobody on the ship had faith?" Laurel inquired.

"That we don't know. As I said before, there are many things that we cannot understand. 'God moves in a mysterious way His wonders to perform.' "

"That's a beautiful out, Aunt Celia." Rome gave her his most charming smile. He turned to Uncle Cam, who was looking through the newspaper. "What do you say?"

"About what? Just been reading about the Panama Canal, a mighty smart thing that is."

"Oh, sure," Rome agreed. "But what we want right now is your philosophy of life—just the subject for a hot night."

Uncle Cam cleared his throat. His blue eyes twinkled behind his spectacles. "All I've got to say is 'Be of good cheer, and I'll be with you.' "

"The palm is yours." Rome rose, gave a little bow, and strolled outside with his pipe.

Laurel longed to follow him, not so much to ask questions as just to be near him in the dark. Instead, she went out on the back porch to sit with Sir Julian until bedtime. Then, lighting the lamp in her room, she held it so Jenny could make her way up the crooked stairs. Jenny was humming *Red Wing* happily. Why did she choose such a sad song? Laurel wondered. Was she somehow boasting of her own good fortune? Her immense satisfaction with life was vaguely annoying. It gave Laurel the feeling of being left out.

Again Jenny did a lot of splashing and scrubbing at the washstand behind the screen. And all the time she chattered. "Mrs. Bowling says she is going to make me some pillow cases and trim them with tatting for my hope chest. Isn't that nice of her? I just know we're going to get along fine. Mama always said you've got to get along with your husband's folks. And everybody here is real friendly and nice, except Edgar doesn't say much. Reckon that's because he's at an age when he doesn't know just where he is. How old are you, Laurel?"

"Fifteen," Laurel said, untying one of her hair ribbons.

"Oh, well, you're not old enough to bother about boys or anything now. Mama always says a girl shouldn't look at a boy until she's at least sixteen, and then just at birthday parties and things like that. And of course she shouldn't let one call on her until she's at least eighteen."

"How about you?" Laurel asked. "Is that the way you did?"

For a moment Jenny didn't answer. There was the sound of water being poured from the bowl into the slop jar. Then she emerged in a long white nightgown with a crocheted yoke. "Well, I may have looked a little harder than Mama thought," she conceded, "but it didn't amount to anything. Now that I'm twenty it all seems a long time ago." She paused to give Laurel a closer look. "You're not interested in boys, are you?"

Laurel removed her other hair ribbon. Certainly she was not interested in boys. Rome was a different matter. He was a man, and what she felt for him was not really what Jenny was talking about. "What on earth makes you think I'd be interested in boys?" she asked.

"Oh, nothing. But you never can tell."

When Laurel had blown out the lamp and they were in bed, Jenny said: "I can't quite figure out that Rome. Reckon artists are always odd people though. He has such a funny way of looking at you."

"What way?" Laurel inquired stiffly.

"A sort of creepy way, makes you feel he wouldn't mind putting his hands on you." Jenny's giggle was a little shrill.

Laurel's body went taut; she couldn't answer.

"Till asleep?"

"No."

"Reckon what I just said sounds silly. Just forget it. Good night."

Forget it, Laurel was thinking, how could you forget a thing like that? She struggled to stop the flow of her imagination. Not Rome and Jenny. Surely he couldn't already be after Jenny, not the way he had been after Sylvia. A tide of sick fear swept over her. Again she could hear Sylvia's laughter in the boxwoods, and, worse still, Sylvia's silence. Again she saw Devoe striding across the yard and through the garden gate.

The following morning her sick fears of the night before seemed foolish and far away. At breakfast Uncle Walter announced his plan to take Jenny to see a dairy farm down on the river, and they left soon afterwards. Out on the lawn, Rome resumed his picture of the stable. She was happy seeing him there by himself, absorbed in his work. He belonged only to himself, and perhaps a little bit to her.

Slowly she climbed the stairs to make up his bed. There were so many beds now, that the job of bedmaking seemed interminable—until she reached Rome's room. It was so filled with his presence that she almost blushed as she turned back the covers and lifted the pillows. His big leather suitcase, papered with labels from European hotels, stood open near the front window. She paused, looking at it without touching it. The air was heavy with a blend of oil paint, pipe tobacco, and another odor that must be his shaving lotion. It was familiar and disturbing. A dark red silk robe in a Persian design was flung carelessly over the head of the bed. His cream-colored pajamas lay in a silken pool on the floor. Picking them up, she felt as though her hands were on his flesh.

Suddenly Mrs. Prickett called up the stairs, "Laurel, hurry up and come down here."

For a moment she could not answer. The call was repeated with an addition. "I know you're up there. I want you to help me clean out the pantry."

Laurel groaned. On a morning like this. But she might have expected something of the sort. Now that the blackberry jam was made, it was like Mrs. Prickett to plunge into some new undertaking. Something seemed to be driving her from the inside. What was it?

With deliberate care she finished putting Rome's room to rights and went on to give the boys' room a lick and a promise as Brindy would say. Then she went down to the kitchen door and called out, "I've still got to make the beds in Uncle Cam's room."

The banging and rustling in the pantry stopped for a moment. "For mercy's sake, don't dawdle so." She could tell by the tone that Mrs. Prickett's face was red, the perspiration standing out on her upper lip and forehead.

She couldn't resist asking, "Why don't you sit on the porch and rest? It must be over ninety."

"Rest!" Mrs. Prickett snorted. "Who has time to rest?"

Laurel did not waste her breath to reply. The answer of course was that Uncle Cam did. She found him near the door of his little house, his chair tilted back against the trunk of an old locust. He was reading a copy of *A Tale of Two Cities* that had been on his mantelpiece since his last visit. With a sigh, she dropped down on the doorstep. "I'm tired," she told him. "I wish Mrs. Prickett would leave."

"Shucks, wouldn't that give you more to do than ever?"

"No, it wouldn't. We'd get Brindy back, and everything would be all right."

He chuckled. "Reckon I know what you mean. Fact is Mrs. Prickett got after me yesterday. Wanted me to learn how to put new cane bottoms in some old chairs here in the loft."

"What did you say?"

"Said I just couldn't break my record." Holding his book in his left hand with one finger marking the place, he looked thoughtfully at his right hand, first the back, then the palm.

Much diverted, Laurel asked, "What record?"

"I am a retired gentleman. For me to work would be a reflection on me and my relations." His gentle blue eyes sparkled with merriment.

Laurel laughed. "Wish I could think of something like that. I could say I am too young to work. The trouble is I am fifteen."

He surveyed her for a moment. "Fifteen. Your great-grandmother was married at fifteen."

"Married?" Even in her imagination, she hadn't gone as far as that. Could a girl of her age actually get married? Somehow she still chose to regard marriage as remote. Somewhere over the hills beyond love. Love was the important thing. Love was enough. She glanced in the direction of the lawn, where Rome was painting. But the white lilac hedge and the huge cedars at the lower end of the front yard obscured her view.

"Got a beau?"

"Of course not."

"Anyhow, 'pears you got ideas."

Gan called from the window of her room, "Laurel, Mrs. Prickett is screaming. See what's the matter. You can get there before I can."

As she rounded the wing formed by Gan's room, she could hear Mrs. Prickett. She sounded as if she had discovered a moccasin snake in the house. Bounding up the kitchen steps, Laurel rushed into the pantry. There lay Mrs. Prickett beside an overturned chair. She lay in the narrow aisle between the shelves, and the flour and sugar barrels. She had lost her glasses and was fumbling helplessly about the vinegar jug.

"Laurel, Laurel, is that you? Merciful heavens, my leg!" She groaned.

"What happened?"

"Can't you see? I fell. I was trying to reach the top shelf—somebody's spilled something on it. When I tried to grab it, my hand slipped off. Here, help me up."

Laurel took her hands and pulled. As she reached a sitting position, she cried out again, "My leg! Mercy, I can't get up. Call Rome."

Laurel restored her glasses, which were fortunately not broken, and ran out to the front porch. Her call to Rome was frantic. She saw the surprised jerk of his head, then he was running across the lawn toward her. When they got to the pantry, Gan was there, and Uncle Cam was entering the kitchen.

"Help me to my room," Mrs. Prickett was demanding, "help me to my room."

"Just a minute," Rome said, kneeling beside her. As he ran his hands over her right leg, she gave a cry.

"I think it's broken," he said quietly. "We'd better not move you till the doctor comes."

"Merciful heavens, oh, merciful heavens!"

Laurel had never expected to see Mrs. Prickett look so dismayed, so fearful. Gan turned to Laurel. "Run to the stable, dear. Tell Billy to ride up to Mr. Giffin's and phone for Dr. Walton."

"You ought to have a phone here," Rome said severely.

"Yes, I know." Gan's voice was agitated. "We would except for Margaret and the trees."

Laurel did not wait to hear the familiar explanation. Her sympathies were entirely with Mother in the matter. She, too, loved the beautiful young cedars that bordered the road leading toward Cool Hill and Pigeon Run. The telephone company had insisted it would have to lop them off on one side if it put up a line. This, Mother had maintained, would be worse than murder. Since the Blue Ridge View property extended for a mile in that direction, Papa had considerable influence in the situation. There was also a network of political relationships involving Mr. Giffin, who was the road supervisor, and the head of the company, in which Papa held some kind of ace. The upshot was that Blue Ridge View had no phone, but the avenue of cedars marched, happy and undisturbed, along the road.

When she announced that Mrs. Prickett had broken her leg, Billy showed no surprise at all. "Might have figured," he said, "it'd either be that or her neck."

chapter

11

IT WAS two and a half hours before Dr. Walton got there, driven in his Ford runabout by a young colored man. The doctor maintained that he didn't have time to learn to drive himself, and besides he needed the opportunity to relax between calls. He was a pale immaculate man, who carried himself slightly hunched. A drooping black mustache gave him an enigmatic expression. He said little, but had a talent for looking profound. His comments on a patient's condition were rare. He wrote his prescriptions in a galloping scrawl that was illegible to every one except old Mr. Reeves, who ran the drugstore at Pigeon Run.

He showed no surprise at finding Mrs. Prickett on the

pantry floor with a pile of pillows at her back. He placed his white panama on the flour barrel and knelt beside her to make his examination. Laurel waited in the kitchen with Rome and Gan. She felt greatly subdued and vaguely conscience stricken at the sight of Mrs. Prickett lying in defeat beneath the unstraightened pantry shelves. Still she hadn't really wanted anything like this to happen, she had merely wished she would leave. And, even if she had hurried faster through her bedmaking that morning and gone to help Mrs. Prickett, the fall would have probably taken place just the same. As Billy said, it might have been her neck. Lucky it was just her leg.

By the middle of the afternoon, Mrs. Prickett was ensconced in Mother's bed with her right leg in a splint, and a high thing like a gallows rigged up to maintain traction. She was still dozing from the effects of the chloroform and looked more peaceful than Laurel had ever seen her. Dr. Walton had left with Gan a bottle of what he called pain pills. Mother's room was filled with the disquieting scent of iodoform, and the house as a whole reminded her of the way things were after a big thunderstorm—a strange unearthly stillness.

Gan, looking flushed and worried, called Laurel into her room. Her white hair had strayed from her side combs, and her little white apron, usually so crisp, was crumpled and limp. She sat down heavily in her cane bottom rocker. "Laurel, I want you to go down and see if you can get Brindy back. If she won't come, I don't know what on earth we are going to do."

Running down the lane toward Brindy's cabin, Laurel thought uneasily of Gan. Because of her size, she could not be on her feet too much. Besides she could not stand heat. It would be unthinkable for her to attempt to do the cooking.

Brindy's unpainted cabin was weathered to a pleasant silvery gray. It had a lean-to kitchen and a chimney built of fieldstone. It faced a wild plum thicket and near the door were a few flowers: portulaca, hollyhocks, marigolds, and a lilac bush.

Laurel ran up the three steps and knocked at the half open door. Brindy appeared in a checked gingham dress and a faded apron. "Laurel, my, my! Come right in."

Laurel took the rocking chair she pointed out near the cold fireplace, and knowing it was first necessary to gain Brindy's interest, exclaimed, "We've had a terrible accident!"

"Horse kicked that Edgar, I bet."

"No. And the house is full of company. Uncle Walter's girl, Jenny, is there, and—and Edgar's brother. Besides Uncle Cam's back."

"My, my," Brindy repeated. "Mighty big crowd to cook for." She leaned forward. "Don't tell me Roy or Chris got hisself drownded."

Laurel shook her head. "Nobody's dead, but she might as well be as far as the housework goes."

"It ain't Mrs. Bowling!"

"Gan's all right except she's upset, and you know she can't stand summer heat." She paused, seeing that Brindy was curious but on guard.

"Well, if nobody's dead, reckon I don't have to get myself all riled up."

Laurel plunged. "Mrs. Prickett fell down in the pantry and broke her leg."

There was a flicker in Brindy's eyes, but her expression didn't change. "Now ain't that too bad."

"It's awful—there's nobody to cook. We had cold light bread and fried eggs for dinner."

"Ain't that too bad," Brindy repeated in exactly the same tone.

"So you see we're bad off," Laurel pursued in a woebegone voice.

"Reckon so." Brindy reached up and caught a fly.

Laurel found she didn't want to play the game any longer.

"Oh, Brindy, won't you please, please come back? You know we miss you. You know we didn't want you to leave."

"Did *she* send for me?"

"Oh, no, she's in bed, still in a daze from the medicine and everything. Gan sent for you. She isn't able to cook, she just isn't able."

"What about you?" Brindy asked slyly. "Looks to me like you're able."

"You know I can't cook, Brindy. Besides nobody in the world can cook as well as you."

"Not even *her?*" Brindy inquired, again refusing to use Mrs. Prickett's name.

"Of course not. You're the best cook in the world, that's what Papa always says."

Brindy threw the crumpled fly into the fireplace, folded her arms across her breast and leaned back in a contemplative attitude. She was softened, Laurel hoped, but still unconverted. There must be something else to say, something that would make it easy for Brindy. Suddenly she saw what it was. "You know something, Brindy? I know very well you always do as you please. Mrs. Prickett didn't make you leave, you just quit because you wanted to."

Brindy nodded vigorously. "That's the truth, Laurel. Sure I quit. Didn't have to take no lip off *her*."

"And," Laurel continued, "she can't stop you if you want to come back."

Brindy's lips parted in a slow smile. "That she can't."

Laurel returned in triumph to tell Gan that Brindy would be there to get supper. Jenny and Uncle Walter were back, and Jenny was full of solicitude for Mrs. Prickett, fussing about the bedroom, bathing her face, cleaning her glasses, and seeing that everything she might want was arranged on the table at her side. Laurel saw with sudden clarity that sometime in the future Jenny would be just as busy and bossy a housekeeper as Mrs. Prickett herself. She also saw that Uncle Walter, lost in the world of his dairy barn, would not notice or care. And is that, she asked herself wonderingly, what makes a happy marriage?

She wondered again later that afternoon when she heard Rome in the yard comparing Jenny to a pink peony. Jenny gave a high self-conscious little laugh and said, "Walter never gives me any sweet talk like that."

"I'll have to give him lessons," Rome told her.

Laurel jumped up from her bench in the boxwoods, where she had retreated to rest after the excitement of the day, and ran out into the hot sun of the garden. She could not bear to hear any more. At the far corner, beyond the cucumber rows, she saw Chris, his butterfly net over his shoulder, climbing the fence into the graveyard.

She ran across to him. "What are you going in there for?"

"Shhhhh. I saw a great spangled fritillary light on Uncle Baldwin's tombstone."

She watched him leap into the tangle of myrtle and creep toward the butterfly. She wondered vaguely how it could be so important to him, so unimportant to her. She could think only of Rome, of Rome back there saying those things to Jenny. All the time, with the top of her mind, she was following Chris's progress through the myrtle and wild honeysuckle.

"You're walking on Grandfather's grave," she called out.

He turned to glare at her angrily and tap his lips. The fritillary was still communing with a patch of lichens on the tombstone, its wings moving rhythmically up and down. Just as he raised his net it fluttered away to land high on a yew tree. "It's your fault," he lamented. "What does Grandfather care if I walk on his grave?"

"It didn't hear me," she countered. "Butterflies don't have ears." It was a guess, but she left him considering it, and wandered back toward the wide grassy walk that bisected the garden. When she reached the boxwoods she paused, but today there was no peace in this haven of soft greens and browns, no pleasure in the cool brown earth sifted over with the small brown leaves of the boxwoods that had fallen long ago. Her eyes fell on the mossy bench where Rome and Sylvia might have been sitting the day Devoe found them. She shied away from the scene, tried to submerge herself in the soft gray mists of unknowingness. Then she heard Jenny's laugh, higher and shriller than before. She forced herself to walk out, to pass by them as they sat in the hammock under the locust trees. Uncle Walter had brought out the mower and was cutting grass on the other side of the brick walk. He didn't seem to be paying any attention to them.

"So the dryad emerges," Rome said lazily. "Where've you been, Laurel?"

"To the graveyard," she answered shortly.

"Really? I suppose it does have the advantage of being cool on a day like this. What else did you have in mind?"

He was teasing her, she thought angrily, treating her as if she were a child like Roy or Chris. She replied with haughtiness, "I was deciding where I wanted to be placed."

"And none too soon when one considers your tottering old age."

"Stop all that foolishness," Jenny cried. "It gives me the creeps."

Involuntarily, Laurel blurted out, "You don't look very pale, you still look like a pink peony."

Rome's eyes flickered. He gave her a funny little look. "And what flower would you like to be compared to?"

She did not answer. She ran through the opening in the lilac hedge and left them there. With sudden horror she knew that she had acted like a baby, that she had betrayed herself to Rome.

That night after a supper on which Brindy outdid herself, they gathered as usual in the hall. On account of the heat, the door to Mother's room was wide open, and Mrs. Prickett, now fully alert, watched them from the gallows-like framework that held her leg. She no longer looked defeated, but somehow enthroned. Gan had given her a little silver bell to ring whenever she needed service.

Exhausted by the day's activity, Gan was not playing the piano tonight. She glanced up from reading a letter of Mother's and remarked, "They've been to Mozart's house in Salzburg."

"Saw it the summer I was there to attend the music festival," Rome said. "Picturesque old city, Salzburg."

Laurel eyed him with painful humility. So he had been to Salzburg. Even the name was strange to her.

Edgar hauled in his feet and sat forward in his chair. "Say, Rome, I'd still like to see New York. When are you going to invite me up there like you promised?"

"Oh, someday, fellow. I haven't forgotten."

"Maybe when you go back? Maybe this summer?"

"Maybe."

Laurel felt a stab of envy. The thought of Edgar going off to New York with Rome while she was left alone here was intolerable. She said with intensity: "I wish I could see New York."

Edgar gave a disgusted little laugh. "You don't think Rome would want to be bothered with a girl, do you?"

Rome smiled at her. "I can't imagine that Laurel would ever be a bother." There was a new inflection in his voice.

She sat mute. What was he thinking? Was he remembering how she had betrayed herself that afternoon? Confusion filled her, and a nameless fear.

chapter 12

THE NEXT morning right after breakfast, Mrs. Prickett's little bell began to peal loudly and persistently, and Laurel went in to see what was the matter. Mrs. Prickett sat propped up against pillows, no doubt arranged by Jenny. Her hair was neatly combed and she was wearing her glasses. She held a tablet in one hand and a pencil in the other. "Laurel," she said, "will you please get Brindy, and Chris and Roy?"

Brindy and the boys came, stood in a solemn row at the foot of the bed. They had a subdued air, but Laurel thought that they also looked watchful.

"My accident," Mrs. Prickett announced, "is not going to interfere with my running this household. Mr. and Mrs.

Carlton left me here to look after things, and I intend to do so until they get back."

She tore off a sheet of the lined tablet paper and handed it to Brindy. "Here is a list of what you are to have for dinner and supper today. Each morning I'll give you a new list."

"Yessum," Brindy said, glancing at the paper.

"Today," Mrs. Prickett continued, "I had planned to wash up the dining room and kitchen. I want you to do that. The pantry shelves will have to wait until tomorrow."

"Yessum," Brindy repeated without comment and left.

Mrs. Prickett turned to the boys. "Now I want you two to gather the vegetables every morning as usual. Bring them in here and show them to me. The corn is about gone, but I know we have tomatoes, beets, snaps, carrots, and potatoes. Get tomatoes instead of cucumbers today. Run along."

Drawing a sealed letter out of the tablet, she handed it to Laurel. "Please take this to the mailbox. I want my son to know what has happened. Of course he can't come because the children have measles."

Laurel wanted to say something sympathetic, but before she could speak, Mrs. Prickett went on, "Remember the beds are your job. And be sure to sweep the bedrooms when necessary. Also, help Brindy. Especially with the dishes. I want you to keep on washing the dishes." Mrs. Prickett eyed her meaningfully, no doubt recalling the lettuce leaves she had found floating in Brindy's dishpan.

Laurel was tempted to ask, "Can't you think of something else?" but somehow the sight of the scaffolding that held Mrs. Prickett's leg stilled her tongue.

After she had mailed the letter, she went to the kitchen, where Gan had been putting the food away and stacking the dishes. Looking from Brindy to Laurel, she said, "Well, I suppose poor Mrs. Prickett has told you what she wanted you to do."

"She told us," Brindy said.

Gan leaned against the kitchen table and wiped the per-

spiration off her forehead with her tatting trimmed handkerchief. "We shall all have to do our best," she said. Her eyes
were on Laurel. "We don't want your father and mother to
break up their trip and come home, do we?"

"Of course not," Laurel cried, appalled at the thought.

"It would be a living shame," Brindy mumbled. "Might be
they'll never get another chance to see the Old Country.
'Bout the last thing Miss Margaret said to me was, 'Brindy, at
last I'm going to see the Alhambra in Spain.' "

Chris, who was lingering on the porch with the vegetable
basket in his hand, called out, "We'll be good, Gan."

"How do you know I will?" Roy emerged from the pantry
munching a bacon and biscuit sandwich. Glancing at Gan,
he added, "Oh, well, I will, too."

When the boys had gone out, Gan stood for a moment in
silence, her forehead wrinkled in an unaccustomed frown. At
last she cleared her throat and said slowly, "Mrs. Prickett has
told me that she will try to manage things from her bed. But
she takes her responsibility very seriously." Gan hesitated,
again wiped her face. Dropping her voice, she concluded, "If
there is any trouble, she may think it is her duty to write
them about her accident."

Laurel felt a sudden chill. So that was the stinger. All
along she had had the feeling that Mrs. Prickett would know
how to get her way even now. She had threatened Gan. Rage
shook her. Then a fierce protective love for Gan surged up in
her heart. It wasn't right for her to be caught in the middle
this way, and Papa and Mother wouldn't like it either. She
cried angrily, "She'd better not write them!"

"That's not the right spirit, dear. We must all be patient."
She added, "Fortunately, Jenny has promised to stay and
wait on Mrs. Prickett."

"All summer?" Laurel couldn't keep the dismay out of her
voice.

"I suppose so. It may take longer than that for Mrs. Prickett's leg to mend. Bones knit slowly at her age."

Laurel was silent, knowing that Jenny would in some way bring disaster. First Sylvia and Rome. Now Jenny and Rome. Of course Jenny was not absolutely lost in a cloud of love like Sylvia. Yet Laurel knew something could happen. And there was nothing she could do about it. Uncle Walter was blind. He was always leaving her to go and milk, to look after the cows, to horn in on Billy's handling of the horses, to help Booker harvest his hay or cultivate the garden. It seemed enough for him that Jenny was on the place, where he could see her at mealtime and take her strolling in the evening.

That same afternoon she saw Jenny on the lawn looking over Rome's shoulder as he painted. She herself had not looked at his picture of the stable. She was afraid he might have given it the same sinister quality that he had given Sheep Rock, and she did not want to think of the stable that way. She could not tell what Jenny thought. She just seemed interested. Too interested.

That night in bed Laurel asked her, "How do you like Rome's picture?"

"Oh, I don't know much about painting. It doesn't look like any picture I ever saw though; it doesn't look like the stable either." She added thoughtfully, "I reckon painters are different from other folks. That Rome is something." She giggled.

Laurel thrust her fist against her heart. She had to quiet its beating or Jenny would hear. "You think he's good-looking?"

"Sure he's good-looking. If I was blind in one eye and couldn't see out of the other, I'd know that."

"You—you like him?"

Jenny turned over the other way. "It's so hot, let's throw the sheet back."

"I don't care. You like him, don't you?"

"Oh, I like him all right."

"Does he still make you feel that funny way you said—as if he wanted to put his hands on you?"

"For heaven's sake, Laurel, what a memory you've got. I believe you like him yourself."

Laurel bit her lip. She couldn't let anyone find out, not when she didn't know how Rome felt about her. She answered deviously, "I reckon I like all relatives a little." But she did not press Jenny further. Instead, she kept her eyes open the next day, and the days that followed. And she tried to avoid Rome. She couldn't risk giving herself away again.

One day Edgar ran into her on the back porch and said with a snicker, "You can't fool me, Miss Smarty, you're mad with Rome because he likes Jenny. You're jealous."

Unable to keep the blood from flooding her face, she glared at him furiously. Inside she was filled with shock, dismay. She hadn't imagined that any one would find out her secret, least of all Edgar. Blindly, irrationally, she struck out at him. "It's just too bad you weren't on the *Titanic*."

Almost imperceptibly, he shied back. It was as though the blow had been tangible. His dark eyes flashed strangely, and back of the anger in them there was something else. "You should have been on there yourself," he snapped.

She faced him in trembling silence, wondering if he really knew, or if he only guessed.

As if answering her thought, he went on, "You needn't try to get me off the subject. I know you're crazy about Rome. That's why you put your shoes on this summer."

How awful it was to be hit in the face with the truth. The only defense against the truth was some kind of lie, and she wasn't good at lying.

"That's what you think," she countered. "I'm big enough to wear shoes."

"You mean your feet are big enough." He laughed. "Well, I can tell you one thing. To Rome you're just a kid."

In her heart, this was what she was really afraid of. There had been times when she felt he considered her grown-up, or almost grown-up. And at other times he had aroused her doubts. She couldn't tell whether he couldn't make up his

115

mind, or whether he was just teasing her. She demanded curtly, "Is that what Rome said?"

He shrugged. "Don't you wish you knew?"

"I don't care."

"Then why did you get so mad when I said you were jealous of Jenny?"

That again. He must not see her anger, her fear. "Silly, what do I care about Jenny? If anybody's jealous, it ought to be Uncle Walter."

"Don't worry. Someday he'll notice. Hope I'm around when he does. You'll see some fireworks."

The floor began a gentle quivering as Gan came out of her room and started across to the kitchen. She paused to smooth Laurel's hair back from her forehead. "What are you children so excited about? Isn't it time for you to be on your rounds, Edgar, dear?"

"Yes, Aunt Celia, I'm just leaving." Looking at her, he became a different person. "I'm going to Forest Mill," he added. "Want me to bring you anything from the store?"

"You might get me two or three nutmegs."

"All right. Wouldn't you like to have some horehound candy?"

"That's a thoughtful boy, it would be nice." She patted his shoulder.

Laurel was momentarily diverted from her turmoil. It never ceased to fill her with amazement that any one could be fond of Edgar. Only Gan would be capable of it.

Roy came running through the hall with the mail, thrust it into Gan's hands, and went skipping down the back steps.

"Here's a letter for your Uncle Cam. From Richmond. Must be his pension check."

"I'll take it to him," Laurel offered. "I was just going to make up the beds out there."

She found Uncle Cam in an old rocking chair, which he had placed so as to benefit by the shade of the boxwoods, as well as by the old locust tree beside his house. He rocked

116

gently, his little white beard pointing down to the pages of his novel. When she laid the letter on the open book, he glanced at it, then up at her with a delighted smile. "Thought it was 'bout time my pension was coming. Have to go up to Pigeon Run tomorrow and get it cashed."

When he started off the next morning on Jezebel, as Billy had nicknamed his old pacer, Gan shook her head. "I'm afraid he'll waste all his money before he gets back."

"You mean he'll drink it up," Uncle Walter said bluntly. "Shhh. I hope not."

After that the day went on as usual, and everybody seemed to forget Uncle Cam. But she could not. Even when he failed to return for supper, no one seemed disturbed. "He's probably spending the night with an old crony at Pigeon Run," Gan said. "You know how he is about coming and going."

However, Laurel was not satisfied. Suppose old Jezebel got scared by a car and threw him. Suppose at this very moment he was lying unconscious in a ditch. She had a strong conviction that if Papa had been there he would have gone to see about Uncle Cam. The next morning when he still hadn't returned, she went down to the stable and tried to get Billy to go and look for him. "No use to bother about your Uncle Cam," he said with a cynical wink, "he's on a spree."

This only served to make her more uneasy. Crossing the lawn again, she saw that Byron was still waiting for Edgar. Saddled and tied to the yard fence, he was stamping about and switching his tail restlessly. He looked around at her and gave a questioning whinny. The answer to his question had already sprung into her mind. After a quick glance toward the house, she untied him and jumped on. He gave her only a token nip on the ankle, and they were loping toward the big gate. As she leaned over to slide back the latch, he snorted impatiently. At last it was done. They were outside, galloping up the red clay road, now packed almost to the consistency of marble.

As the wind sang in her ears, she grew conscious of the

beauty of the morning. Larks were singing; the scent of wild honeysuckle filled the air. Mother's young cedar trees marched in proud lines on either side of her. They passed Cool Hill and the colored Baptist church standing serene among its oak trees, then the cross-roads and the turning that took you to the river. Dashing by Mr. Giffin's house, she was reminded of how Papa had once said with a chuckle: "He built close to the road so he could keep an eye on county politics."

Later as they went through a woodland area, she slowed Byron down, remembering that he must not be overheated in this weather. She had been watching for Uncle Cam, but had not stopped to make inquiries. As last, seeing Tyler Morgan beating happily away on his anvil, his old black hat on the back of his head, she drew up. Tyler had seen him go by yesterday morning all right. In fact, he had stopped and passed the time of day, but he hadn't been seen returning.

Byron shied when they met the doctor's car and almost shook her feet out of the stirrups. Otherwise, she arrived at the village without trouble. She tied him near Odlum and Blount's under the same tree where she had waited for Rome. Glancing ruefully down at her rumpled dress, she pushed the hair out of her eyes and summoned enough courage to enter the store. She walked by the caged-off corner at the left, where Miss Daisy Sutton was sorting the mail. Gradually her eyes grew used to the semi-dusk, and she peered about at the loungers grouped from habit around the cold stove, where a carpet of hounds had to be avoided both summer and winter. Uncle Cam was not there. Mr. Odlum, a keen-looking dark little man, who always wore a derby, came forward. "Morning, Miss Carlton. Can I wait on you?"

Barely conscious of the flattering "Miss Carlton," she shook her head. "Not today, thank you. Have—have you seen Uncle Cam?"

He turned to straighten some trace chains suspended from the ceiling. "Did see him around. Can't say where he is now."

"Thanks, Mr. Odlum." She marched on past the candy counter and the yard goods section to the door that looked out on the railroad and the rest of the village. At the station stood a group of people waiting for the morning train. She recognized Miss Alicia Parks, bound no doubt for Lynchburg and her weekly singing lesson. And there of course was Mrs. Wilkens, wife of the station agent, who was said to make use of her free pass every day or so. Then she saw someone else. Uncle Cam came out of the waiting room, zigzagging as though he were dancing to a very slow waltz.

Slowly she went down the path, watching him with a sort of awful fascination. Suddenly he seized Mrs. Wilkens and began whirling her about. He was singing:

"Hop light, ladies, the cake's all dough,
Don't you mind the weather so the wind don't blow."

The pink roses on her hat bobbed ludicrously. She tried to escape. But he held her tighter and quickened his tempo. "Mike," Mrs. Wilkens screamed, "Mike!"

As Mr. Wilkens appeared at the door in shirt sleeves and suspenders, his official cap on the back of his head, Uncle Cam released his flustered wife, bowed gracefully, and seized Miss Alicia Parks. Miss Alicia had been the belle of Pigeon Run for several years, but recently the rumor had gotten out that she was a ruthless mimic. This had somewhat quieted the ardor of suitors and put the townspeople on their guard. Now there was a burst of vengeful delight as she was forced to whirl madly around on the cinders, her skirts flying, her hat slipping over one ear, her music roll sailing into the crowd.

Loud guffaws drowned out her cries. Someone shouted, "Go it, go it, trip the light fantastic!"

Laurel had never in her life felt so humiliated. She glanced wildly about for a place to hide. Old Jeb, leaning on his baggage truck, reminded her of the freight room. But somehow she could not bring herself to retreat. Jeb, she saw, was not laughing. He was watching, but his face was closed, immobile. She wondered if he knew how she felt.

Mercifully, the train blew just then. The great black snout nosed into view. The ground began to shake beneath her. The engine rumbled by, the drivers revolving slower and slower. There was a grinding jerk; the train, with its two red coaches and baggage car, had come to a halt.

Miss Alicia tore herself from Uncle Cam, snatched up her music roll, and sprang onto the steps before the brakeman could put down the stool.

Thankful for the diversion, Laurel, for once unmindful of the train, grabbed Uncle Cam by the arm and pulled him behind the station and into the baggage room.

"Take here," he objected, "take here!"

But by the time he could free himself from her grasp they were well inside. "What you want to bother me for?" he cried angrily. "Just having a little fun."

"Sit down," she begged desperately, "sit down and rest."

The train pulled out, and Old Jeb wheeled in his truck load of baggage. "Howdy, Miss Laurel," he said as if there were nothing unusual about the situation. "I got a pot of coffee on my little stove back there. Maybe Mr. Cam'd like to have a cup."

"No," he yelled.

But when Jeb placed the cup of coffee in his hands he began drinking it. Then Jeb produced a pone of corn bread and handed it to him without comment.

Gradually Uncle Cam subsided on a trunk; his flushed cheeks and red nose grew paler. Holding her breath, Laurel watched the change. With repugnance he began nibbling at the bread, then Jeb brought the coffeepot and refilled his cup. Aside to her he said, "Don't you worry. He'll be hisself 'fore you know it."

Uncle Cam was not exactly himself when they left sometime later, but he was able to walk without waltzing. The trouble was he couldn't remember where he'd tied the old pacer. "Could swear she was near the drugstore," he muttered.

"If she broke loose, she certainly didn't come home."

"She's always hungry. Reckon maybe—"

Somebody's garden, she thought with alarm. Her deduction proved correct. They located Jezebel in Mr. Reeve's immaculate garden behind the drugstore. She was making the most of the corn patch. Mr. Reeves rushed out, his little eyes darting wrathfully above the hay bundle of his beard.

Laurel reached out cautiously to grasp the bridle. Jezebel backed her ears and bared her teeth.

"Watch out," Uncle Cam warned.

Laurel's impulse was to turn and run. But she controlled herself, called out a loud "Whoa," and seized the dragging reins.

Mr. Reeves' beard shook with his muttering. Then it stopped shaking. He grumbled, "If it was anybody but John Carlton's folks, I'd make you pay damages."

"Not much damage," Uncle Cam soothed, "not much damage."

"Thank you, Mr. Reeves," Laurel said. "I'll tell Papa."

Side by side she and Uncle Cam rode out of town in the noonday heat. She was beginning to think uneasily of what she would have to face when she got home. Except for running away a few times when she was small, and then only to Forest Mill or Cool Hill, she had never left home on her own initiative before. Edgar would be furious because she had dared to take Byron, and Gan—Gan could be very stern when she felt duty was involved.

chapter
13

AS SOON as they reached home, Gan called Laurel into her room. Gan's cheeks were very pink, her lips set in a firm line. She sat straight in her cane-bottom chair, while Laurel remained standing. From above the corner mantelpiece the portrait of Gan's youngest sister, Flora, the mother of Edgar and Rome, looked down at them. Her face was calm and sweet, somehow untouched. It had been taken when she was eighteen, before the troublesome period of her marriage. But Laurel was not thinking of Flora now, she was thinking of Gan, who always held a central place in her firmament. In some strange way, offending Gan was a punishment in itself.

"Laurel," Gan said, "you have been disobedient. You have

been told never to leave home without permission."

"But what about Uncle Cam? I was afraid—"

"Your Uncle Cam is old enough to look after himself. He is not your responsibility. But you are my responsibility. You seem to forget that."

"But I'm older now, I'm old enough to ride to Pigeon Run."

"Astride," Gan said as though she were pronouncing a sentence of doom. "You have disgraced us all."

It sounded so terrible when Gan said it that Laurel was suddenly shocked at herself. "I had on bloomers," she pointed out, "to match my pink chambray dress."

"No matter, you rode astride. No lady would do such a thing."

Since she had been trying so hard to convince herself and others that she was grown-up, this comment was a painful blow. While she was trying to think of a suitable reply, there was a sharp peal from Mrs. Prickett's little bell.

"Oh, dear." Gan rose. "Jenny is out with Walter, and Brindy never hears."

Laurel followed her through the little passage connecting her room with Mrs. Prickett's. It contained cupboards and the dark closet under the crooked stair that wound up to Laurel's room.

Mrs. Prickett was still ringing, her eyes darting from one door to the other. "Oh, Mrs. Bowling, I wanted to see you about Laurel. I hope you have punished her properly. If there's one thing I can't tolerate, it's a wayward girl."

Gan stiffened. "Mrs. Prickett, I do not care for the use of that word in connection with my granddaughter."

"If the cap fits, let her wear it."

Laurel had not often seen Gan angry, but she was angry now. "Laurel has been disobedient, but she has not been wayward. I'll thank you to withdraw that word." There was something majestic about Gan as she stood there. She seemed taller; her eyes were blazing.

In her excitement over the conflict, Laurel almost forgot that she herself was the cause of it. As she well knew, Mrs. Prickett was not one to back down. She feared for Gan because she was so peace-loving. She could not bear to see her beaten.

Then she saw that Gan's look had the wrath of God in it, and apparently Mrs. Prickett saw it, too, for she said, "Wayward or naughty, what's the difference? You will certainly agree that she has been naughty."

Gan let out her breath slowly, her eyes quieted. "Yes, she has been naughty, and I have every intention of punishing her. Come, Laurel."

In the passage she pointed to the stairs. "Go to your room, you will live on bread and water for the rest of the day."

The penalty was unpleasant and humiliating, but Laurel felt it could have been worse. Gan had not sent for a peach tree switch, and she had not bolted her in the dark closet as Mother had done on various occasions. Either of these things would have made it impossible for her ever to face Rome again. Restlessly she moved about in the stupefying heat, wondered if he would miss her at supper, if he would ask for her.

After a while she heard heavy clumping footsteps on the stairs, then a loud knock on the door. Puzzled, she opened it.

"Heh," Edgar growled, "what you mean by taking my horse? You've cost me a sale. Tom Higgins was going to buy the *Titanic* book this morning before he left for Roanoke."

She was conscious of the genuine disappointment that underlay the gruffness in his voice, but she ignored it and sprang to her own defense. "Byron's Papa's horse. I reckon I've got a right to ride him sometimes."

His eyes clouded. "Why didn't you ask ahead? You didn't have to sneak off with him."

Something in his tone caused her anger to subside. "I didn't know I was going to do it. I—I had to find Uncle Cam."

He raked one foot back and forth, leaned against the door jamb. "Say, what was he up to?"

"Oh, he was at Pigeon Run. Old Jezebel had broken loose and gotten into Mr. Reeves' garden."

"Ha, ha! Bet that wasn't all."

"I found Jezebel," she went on, "then we came home."

He shrugged. "You don't have to cover up for him. Everybody knows what he was doing."

She was silent.

He continued, "He's out there in his house sleeping it off. You'd think he was old enough to know better."

"Let him alone," she said fiercely. "He was just trying to have a little fun, he wasn't hurting anybody." In her defense of him she had forgotten her own humiliation, her own anger at Uncle Cam.

"Don't get sore at me, I haven't done anything to him." Edgar turned and clumped downstairs.

It was nearly supper time when Jenny came running up the steps, humming *Red Wing* again. "I'll bet you've been roasting," she said cheerfully. "Rome went with Walter and me over to the mill to get some fresh meal. Says he's going to paint the millpond with a body floating in it. That Rome is really something."

"You like him, don't you?"

"Don't know whether I do or not. You never know how to take him." She pulled off her blue-and-white gingham over her head and went to the washstand.

Just the same you can't keep your eyes off him, or your mind, Laurel was thinking. She watched enviously as Jenny put on her clinging green voile. It fitted too well, made her look disgracefully feminine. As she combed it, her thick brown hair seemed to spring into new curls about her pink-and-white face. She was just too healthy, too much alive. "Sorry you can't come down," she said as she left. "I must run and fix Mrs. Prickett's tray."

Laurel refused to say, "What about me?" But she was

getting desperately hungry. The tantalizing smell of frying chicken drifted in through the back window. Earlier she had caught the equally tantalizing fragrance of Brindy's apple pies. When the supper bell rang, she could hardly restrain herself from going down and taking her place at the table. But Gan, she knew, would ask her to leave. And Rome would be there. He would think of her as a child being punished.

The soft slap of bare feet on wood presaged Chris's knock on the door. He handed her a plate bearing one slice of lightbread and a glass of water. "Gan says here's your sup-per." He surveyed her solemnly. "What made you run away to Pigeon Run?"

"I didn't run away, I had to go on business."

He didn't seem satisfied, but he left without further questions. Instantly, she snatched up the bread and ate it, then swallowed the glass of water. She felt even hungrier than before. Her stomach was a pit of emptiness. She began to torture herself further by imagining the platter of fried chicken in front of Uncle Walter.

She didn't hear any sound on the stairs, she only knew Brindy was there when the door opened. "Take this quick," she whispered, " 'for they miss me. Had to creep up so's the old woman below wouldn't catch on."

"Oh, oh!" Laurel's mouth was watering. It was too good to be true; it was like a dream. The tray held fried chicken, hot buttered rolls, corn pudding, milk, and a large slice of apple pie.

"Thank you, Brindy, thank you, thank you!"

"Shhh. Don't say anything. Got to get back. Hide the tray under the bed when you get through." She was gone. Except for one tiny squeak from a stair step, there was no sound.

Laurel set the tray on a table and drew up a chair. Noth-ing in her life had ever tasted so good. Brindy had given her a leg and a breast, and she hadn't forgotten to add a liver and a gizzard. The rolls were saturated with butter, the corn pudding rich with eggs. And the pie! Nobody else in the world could make such crust. When she had finished the last crumb, she was convinced that Brindy deserved nothing less than a throne in heaven.

With a sigh of contentment, she hid the tray and began to think of other things. Jenny had said Rome was going to paint the millpond. She remembered his saying long ago that he didn't intend to paint the mill because too many mills were painted. But the pond was sinister. It was deep and dark and still, with roots and slime at the bottom. Trees made a canopy over it. Occasionally men fished there for eels and perch. Otherwise, the pond was left pretty much to itself. She recalled that Papa had spoken of swimming there as a young man. Even now she shuddered at the thought. Such dark murky water. Anything could be in its depths. Things besides slime and old logs and slithering eels.

She lit the lamp, put on her nightgown, and took down a copy of *Little Dorrit* from the row of books she kept on the mantelpiece. Diverted by little Dorrit's troubles, she could forget her own.

When she went up to make Rome's bed the following morning, she saw the completed picture of the rock stable standing on a chair. At first it seemed beautiful. About the mellowed gold and silver of the stones there was a timeless quality, enhanced by the weather-grayed shingles. Without being able to put it into words, she sensed for the first time that the stable was a human creation that in some degree approached the perfection of a natural creation. Then she realized that the cutting-room door was ajar. In the shadows stood a figure vaguely suggesting Billy. The figure held in its hand an upended pitchfork. Nothing extraordinary. And yet there was something in the dark outlines, in the sharpness of the fork prongs—she could not give it a name. She turned away and removed the faded lilies from a vase on the dressing table.

From the hall below rose a sudden burst of voices. She ran

down the stairs past the landing and saw that Roy had just brought up the mail. Rome stood with a letter in his hand. He looked more pleased than she had ever seen him. Catching sight of her, he waved the letter. "Laurel, my agent likes the picture of Sheep Rock. What do you think of that?"

Before she could answer, he had turned to Gan. "He wants some more things from down here to add to my one-man show this fall."

"That's nice," Gan said with less enthusiasm than Rome was obviously looking for.

He remarked wryly, "Lucky he doesn't share the opinion of the local art critics."

Laurel could think of only one thing. Now he was sure to stay at Blue Ridge View for the rest of the summer.

Uncle Walter was showing Jenny something in the new *Country Gentleman,* but her mind was evidently on Rome's news. Leaving Uncle Walter's side with an absentminded nod, she said, "Well, Rome, I reckon you'll soon be famous, won't you?"

"Oh, it's not so quick and easy as all that, but this fellow Crayton is something to please."

"A show in New York," Jenny said wonderingly. "I certainly would like to see that. Specially with pictures from around here."

Laurel felt annoyed with Jenny for being so impressed. Rome and his paintings were really none of her concern. The next instant she knew that she had decided the matter too soon.

"How would you like to be in one of my pictures and have all New York admiring you?" He was looking at Jenny with a bold challenge in his eyes.

Jenny began fluttering and blushing and acting as if she didn't know what to say or do. "Oh, I'm not pretty enough for that."

He smiled. "I want to paint you, Jenny."

Laurel stood rigid, gripping the banister. There was an

intimacy in his tone that seemed to shut out everyone else in the hall.

Uncle Walter, who had not paid the least attention, touched Jenny's arm. "Look here at this model silo. Sure would like to have it on our place someday."

Rome threw back his head and laughed as she had never heard him laugh before. "Really, Walter, you're incredible—the perfect realist."

Uncle Walter looked at him oddly, a slight frown on his face. "What's so funny?" he demanded. "This is the best silo I ever saw.

"I'm sure it is." Rome left the hall still laughing.

The quarrel came two days later. Up early for once, Rome had gone out before breakfast and asked Billy to hitch up the buggy so he could drive to Forest Mill and start on his new picture. He had his painting equipment piled on the front porch. As they were all leaving the dining room, he said to Jenny, "Hurry up and get your things. I'm ready."

"What in blazes are you talking about?" Uncle Walter wanted to know. "Jenny and I are going over the other side of Pigeon Run to see a prize heifer."

"Why, Walter," Jenny cried, "you didn't tell me!"

"Tell you? I told you Sunday."

"But I'd forgotten. You didn't say it was today."

"You might have figured it was. You know very well I was helping Billy clean out the stable yesterday."

Jenny answered with unusual tartness, "It wouldn't take a detective to find out what you've been doing. Well, I've promised Rome. He's going to put me in his picture." Despite the defiance in her voice, she blushed.

"Not on your life he isn't."

"I'd like to know why not."

They faced each other, their eyes flashing. In the first seconds Laurel was horrified. Then she had a sadistic desire to see the battle run its course.

"For Pete's sake, Walter, be your age," Rome said.

129

"Stay out of this," Uncle Walter growled, "it's none of your business."

"I fail to see that. Jenny's agreed to pose."

Uncle Walter leveled his gaze at her. "When did you agree to any such thing?"

"Don't act as if you never heard of it. We were talking about it right here in the hall the other day."

"I'm not going to stand for it. Get that through your head."

"What's wrong with it?" Her voice quivered with anger.

"I'm not going to have a wife of mine exhibited in any public art gallery."

"I'm not your wife yet."

Ignoring this, he turned to Rome. "You let Jenny alone, understand? Try anything like you tried with Sylvia Leigh, and I'll settle your hash."

At his words there was a sudden stillness in the hall. He never spoke idly, and it was obvious that he was not speaking idly now. Laurel saw that his hard brown hands were clenched; the muscles of his arms bulged. But it was the expression on his face that filled her with foreboding. She was seeing Uncle Walter for the first time.

Rome laughed shortly. "Don't tell me the Dark Ages are back."

chapter
14

IT SEEMED apparent that Uncle Walter had gotten his way. A subdued Jenny went with him on trips to see prize cattle and sometimes accompanied him when he went to the stable to milk.

Acting as though the incident had been of no importance, Rome was working alone on his picture of the millpond. But Laurel could not believe he had given up his original plan to include a figure. She kept recalling his tone, the way he had looked at Jenny—the torment was inescapable.

Some evenings she would go to her room before Jenny, comb out her braids and coil her hair on top of her head, then gaze into the mirror. At such times she assured herself

that she looked as old as Jenny. One night, to test this theory
further, she dared to put on Jenny's green voile dress. She
was walking up and down, swishing her skirts and feeling
herself to be at least eighteen, when she heard Jenny's quick
steps on the stairs. There was no time to get out of the dress.
She stood rock still in the center of the floor, her head high,
her cheeks burning.

Jenny opened the door with a rush, and stared. "Laurel! I
thought for a second it was somebody else."

"I—I hope you don't mind."

"Of course not. I used to dress up when I was a kid."

"But I'm not a kid. The dress fits me."

Jenny scrutinized her. "Well, maybe so, except it's too
long. I do believe you need a corset. Don't have one, do
you?"

Laurel shook her head.

"Oh, well there's plenty of time. You'll be a young lady
soon enough."

Laurel couldn't restrain herself. "What do you think I am
now? My great-grandmother was married at my age."

"I declare. You have got notions. You crazy about some
boy? A boy over at Pigeon Run maybe? Bet that's the reason
you took out after Uncle Cam."

"I should say not!" Laurel unfastened the dress and pulled
it off over her head.

"Then who could it be?"

Laurel felt sudden panic. She had to change the current of
Jenny's thoughts. "If you want to know the truth," she burst
out, "I wish I were grown so I could go to Europe."

"So that's it. I reckon all those letters from your mother
make it sound pretty exciting."

Well, it's true, Laurel told herself. I do want to go someday. But not now, not while Rome is here.

Evidently losing interest in Laurel, Jenny began to un-
dress. She had not referred to the quarrel between Rome and
Uncle Walter, but Laurel was sure it had been on her mind.

Doubtless she had been proud and mad, and a little scared, all at the same time. At any rate, that was the way she herself would have felt. She asked now, partly with the idea of keeping Jenny's mind on her own affairs, "Are you still crazy about Uncle Walter?"

"What a silly question. You know I'm engaged to him. We're going to get married as soon as he finishes college."

"I know all that. But you do still love him for good and all, don't you?"

"Sure I love him. I don't know what's got into you, Laurel."

Laurel couldn't bring herself to say anything about Rome, but Jenny added bluntly, "Don't you pay any attention to what you hear Rome say. It's just his nature to talk that way."

"What way?"

Jenny stopped brushing her hair. "Look here, what business is it of yours? I do believe—"

Laurel didn't let her finish. "Everybody in the house saw them nearly get in a fight over you."

Jenny laughed self-consciously. The sound of her laughter, the brightness of her eyes reflected in the mirror, betrayed her. In spite of her common sense, she had been delighted. This was what Laurel had feared. It could only mean that the matter was not ended.

A few days later she was proved right. One of the tenants came before breakfast and took Uncle Walter back with him to look after a sick horse. About nine, as Jenny was coming out of Mrs. Prickett's room with her tray, Rome said to her casually, "How about riding over to the mill with me? Even if you can't pose, you can look at the picture."

Jenny thought for a moment and glanced at Laurel, who was just starting upstairs with an armful of clean sheets. "All right. Laurel can go, too. I'll make sandwiches for a picnic."

Anxiously, Laurel studied Rome's face. His bright-eyed, smiling expression did not change. "Fine. I'll see what in-

133

ducement Billy requires to hitch up the buggy."

When they had gone, Laurel remained where she was, not knowing whether to be elated or crestfallen.

Edgar, who had been sitting at the desk making out his report for the book company, turned. "So you're going to be a third party," he gibed.

She considered him almost with detachment. As she had grown more and more absorbed in Rome, her perpetual feud with Edgar had subsided. She said shortly, "You heard them ask me. It wasn't my idea."

"Them? You mean Jenny. The only reason she asked you was because she's afraid of Walter. You wouldn't catch me being a third party."

"You weren't asked," she snapped, and ran upstairs to hurry through the bedmaking. She tried not to think of what he had said. But his words stayed with her.

When they went out to the buggy, Rome helped Jenny in first so she would sit in the middle next to him. He allowed the horse to walk down the winding hill toward the covered bridge. Except for the graceful arching of the birch trees, the approaches were open. He stopped the buggy and they listened for a moment in silence to the sound of the creek tumbling over the rocks.

"What are you waiting for?" Jenny asked.

"I'm enjoying the bridge."

I know, Laurel wanted to cry, I always enjoy the bridge.

Jenny moved restlessly. "Whoever heard of enjoying a bridge? Bridges are to use."

"Naturally. Any objection to enjoying them, too?"

"Oh, I guess not."

"Those birches," he said to himself. Then he slapped the reins over Juno's back, and they drove on.

Laurel felt as though she would burst with the desire to say that she understood. But she couldn't find the words. Besides, as she glanced out of the corner of her eye, she saw that Rome's knee touched Jenny's knee, that his shoulder

134

was pressed against hers. Jenny, gazing straight ahead, seemed oblivious to the contact. But she had a relaxed contented look like a cat sitting in someone's lap.

Laurel forced herself to give her attention to the wooded cliff, to Papa's flower garden high on its rocky ledge. Now there were only ferns and heart leaves to adorn it.

"For goodness' sake, Laurel," Jenny said unexpectedly, "has the cat got your tongue?"

Laurel felt a jab of resentment. It was the kind of question a thoughtless grown person asked an embarrassed child. As the question itself once had done, the implication annoyed her. She answered with dignity, "I was admiring the cliff."

Jenny giggled. "You and Rome. I'll have to get all excited over the way the raspberries grow in the ditch."

Laurel was rewarded by a glance from Rome, slightly questioning and not without approval. But he merely said non-committally, "There are all kinds of things to see."

She was hurt, disappointed. He could have said something nice to her; he could have made fun of Jenny. But again she recalled his speech comparing Jenny to a pink peony. She looked down hopelessly at her freshly cleaned white shoes. The little blue flowers in her dress seemed to weave and dance in mockery. She almost wished she had not come.

When they reached the millpond, Rome swung her out just as he did Jenny, and she felt momentarily cheered. While he went into the mill to get his painting things, she and Jenny settled down on a patch of lush green grass that furnished a sharp contrast to the dark water of the pond.

"Oo-oo, I'd hate to fall in there." Jenny shuddered.

Involuntarily, Laurel drew back, her eyes on a half-submerged log that somehow suggested a dead monster. Yet she did not like to admit her fear of the pond. Loving the open running water of the creek as she did, she could not understand this fear and was ashamed of it. She merely said, "Plenty of eels in there."

"Eels? I hate eels. They're nothing but water snakes."

135

Rome came back and set up his easel. "If you girls don't mind, I'll work a while before lunch," he said. When he had started to paint, he seemed to forget them.

After a time, Jenny gave up chattering and said she was going over to the spring for some water. She got a Mason jar from the picnic basket and asked Laurel to go with her. Laurel shook her head. She wanted only to sit there and watch Rome. If he was paying no attention to her, neither did he appear to take any interest in what Jenny was doing. For this little space she could imagine that she possessed him, that they were alone in the world. Alone with the grass and trees, and the steady rumble of the water as it plunged over the dam.

It wasn't until after the picnic lunch that Rome invited them to inspect the picture. The dark trees hovered over the black water of the pond. The half-submerged log was barely sketched in, the area near it blank.

Jenny examined it, her head on one side, a puzzled expression on her face. "I reckon you haven't finished it, have you?" she said at last.

"No, I haven't." For a moment he was silent, then he turned and looked full at her. "The picture is waiting for you, Jenny."

Her eyes lighted, but she answered hesitantly, "I don't really mind being in it, but you know what Walter said."

"Maybe he would change his mind if it turned out well."

She looked doubtful. "I'm afraid he wouldn't."

With a show of indifference, he began lighting his pipe. "Of course if you are afraid of Walter—"

"Of course I'm not afraid of him!"

"Then we'll tackle it."

She was scrutinizing the picture again. Suddenly she demanded, "Where would I be?"

"Oh, you would be the center of interest. I'd call it 'The Drowned Maiden.'"

"Drowned?"

"Yes, you'd be floating face up by the log—no reason why a body shouldn't float in that position."

"In there?" she shrieked. "You mean in that water?"

"Certainly. After all it's summer, the water's warm."

"I wouldn't get in that water for a million dollars."

I know how you feel, Laurel thought. And yet for Rome? Would it be possible to do it for him? If she were in Jenny's place, if she were asked. She didn't know. It would be the hardest thing in the world she could imagine doing, the most terrible. No, it wouldn't be possible, not even for Rome. The very thought of it made her shiver, made the flesh crawl from the soles of her feet clear up through her body.

Rome laughed, though she felt it was a surface laugh. He wanted to hide his disappointment. He didn't want to let Jenny know how much it meant to him to do that picture. "Too bad," he said. "You might have found New York at your feet this fall."

Jenny was making anxious little pleats in the side of her dress, swinging uneasily from one foot to the other. It was obvious that she yearned to be in the painting, but couldn't force herself to pose in the pond.

Rome waited, but not too long. "All right, we'll compromise. Lie on that grass there, and I'll see if I can transpose you to the water."

Jenny relaxed, turned to look down at the grass.

Laurel had the feeling that had he proposed this first, she would have refused. But now, contrasted with getting into the black waters of the pond, it seemed so simple and easy that it was like nothing.

"Unfasten your hair," Rome said, "it must float on the water." He glanced at Laurel. "Honey, will you please put the basket in the buggy?"

Slowly she obeyed, trying to believe that the "honey" had not been entirely casual. Juno was unhitched, standing in relative contentment under the tree. She climbed into the deserted buggy, and sat watching the scene on the bank of

137

the pond only a few yards away. Jenny was stretched out on the ground. Rome knelt beside her arranging her hair.

The miller was grinding now, and, instead of the thunder of the water crashing over the dam, there was only a muted humming.

It was at this moment that Uncle Walter galloped up on Lady. As he jumped off, Rome glanced over his shoulder and got to his feet. Jenny raised her head and screamed.

Laurel did not quite catch what Uncle Walter said, but she distinctly heard Rome cry, "Don't be a fool, Walter!"

Uncle Walter advanced, his head tilted forward, his bare muscular arms crooked, his fists balled up.

Without realizing it, Laurel yelled, "Rome, oh, Rome!"

But instinctively, it seemed, Rome had assumed somewhat the same stance. When Uncle Walter struck, Rome's arm was up in defense.

Jenny screamed again. She was up now, backed against a tree, her long hair swirling about her shoulders.

Walter was a blind blunt force unleashed, a maddened bull. Rome danced and swung with the grace of a wildcat. Laurel had the awful feeling that it could go on forever like that, Uncle Walter lunging furiously, Rome sidestepping and missing most of his blows. At first the rage was all Uncle Walter's. Rome's expression showed disgust and annoyance. Several times he repeated his demand, "Don't be a fool."

But Uncle Walter kept on and gradually a look of anger spread over Rome's face. His eyes sparked dangerously. He was not merely defending himself now, he was making calculated blows. She remembered things Gan had said about Rome's father, that he had had an ungovernable temper, that once he had nearly killed a man.

The thought filled her with horror. In a burst of imagination she saw Gan weeping over Uncle Walter's dead body, and Rome marching to the electric chair, his head held at a proud angle, a defiant glow in his dark eyes. The picture was too real, too vivid. She could not stand it. She had to do something. She thought of jumping on Lady and galloping off, shrieking to attract their attention. Then she realized that it would take more than that to part them. She glanced at Jenny, but Jenny was useless. She was still pressed against the tree, wailing. No, it was up to her, Laurel, to do something. Already she had jumped out of the buggy.

There was just one thing. The very thought chilled her. She wasn't that brave. She had never done anything that brave in her life. But even as she tried to deny her courage, her eyes went in fearful fascination to the millpond, to the black mill water that had always made her shudder. She thought of Mother, who was never timid. If Mother were here, if she were faced with this situation, she would say simply, "It's only water."

Before she could lapse again into her own cowardice, she acted. She rushed forward past the struggling men, and leaped feet first into the pond. The water was ice cold. She was plunging down, down into the dreadful depths. Finally, when she came choking and spluttering to the surface, her arms and legs were too numb to swim. Her cry for help was desperate.

As though they were in another world, she saw Rome and Uncle Walter there on the bank still fighting. They stopped, turned toward her. She cried out once more, sank into the chilling depths.

She came to the surface a second time, gasping for air. Someone seized her. Rome. Rome was there beside her. And Uncle Walter. They had both followed her into the pond. Only when she was safely on the bank, when she had spat out the water, when the stinging in her nose had eased, did she think of the wonder of it.

Uncle Walter was eyeing her severely. "Of all the crazy things, that takes the cake. You came darn near drowning.'

She was silent.

Rome stooped down beside her. "What made you do it?" She looked into his eyes, wordless.

Jenny gave a hysterical laugh. "You never know what Laurel is going to do. Look at the way she ran off after Uncle Cam."

"She doesn't do things without a reason," Rome said. "Maybe she just couldn't stand to see two grown men acting like idiots." He looked hard at Uncle Walter, who was busy wringing the water out of his trouser legs.

"Idiot or no idiot," Uncle Walter growled, "I hope you've learned your lesson."

Rome pushed the wet hair back from his forehead. "I've learned something remarkable, but I'd scarcely call it a lesson." He gave Laurel a smile that sent a tide of warmth through her chilled body.

chapter

15

IT WAS Jenny who made the mistake of telling Mrs. Prickett what had happened at the millpond. Laurel was upstairs putting on dry clothes when she heard their excited voices in the room below. She jerked on her dress and ran down barefooted. Stirring up Mrs. Prickett could only mean trouble. If she couldn't stop it, at least she could find out what was likely to happen. She paused in the open doorway.

Jenny was standing at the foot of the bed waving her arms. "They were just about to kill each other!"

"Why didn't you separate them?" Mrs. Prickett demanded.

"Separate them? I'd like to know how."

"It seems that Laurel found a way."

Jenny's mouth fell open. "She just happened to jump in like any kid because she was ornery."

Mrs. Prickett pursed up her lips. "I'm not so sure she was just ornery that time."

Laurel gave a little exclamation of astonishment, and they both turned. "Eavesdropping," said Mrs. Prickett.

"I wasn't either, I was standing here in plain sight."

Mrs. Prickett didn't pursue the point. "Why did you jump in the pond, Laurel? You might have been drowned."

Laurel faced Mrs. Prickett's glittering glasses and could think of nothing better than repeating Jenny's words: "They were just about to kill each other."

"That wasn't your affair. Suppose you had been drowned? What would I have said to your father and mother?"

"It wouldn't have been your fault."

"I'd have been held responsible. I was left here to look after things and see there wasn't too much strain on Mrs. Bowling."

Laurel listened uneasily.

"Call your grandmother," said Mrs. Prickett.

Reluctantly, she went to find Gan sitting by the kitchen table deviling eggs for Brindy. Without asking questions, she rose, washed her hands, and went with Laurel back to Mrs. Prickett's room.

Mrs. Prickett began at once. "Mrs. Bowling, I reckon you know about that awful thing at the millpond."

"Yes," Gan said sadly, "a quarrel always grieves me."

"It wasn't only a quarrel," Mrs. Prickett answered sharply, "it was a knock-down and drag-out fight. What's more, Laurel might have lost her life."

Gan reached out and drew Laurel to her. "I didn't realize it was that serious."

"Indeed it was. Jenny says she was going down for the third time."

"She certainly was," Jenny broke in. "I thought it was the end."

Laurel didn't interrupt to tell them it was only the second time.

"Something has to be done," Mrs. Prickett said decisively.

"It's all over," Gan pointed out. "I'm sure nothing of the sort will happen again."

"There's bad blood between Walter and Rome. They should not remain under the same roof."

"Surely you are not suggesting, Mrs. Prickett, that I should put out either my nephew or my son." As she spoke, there was a touch of majesty about Gan.

"Yes, I am. Before worse happens." Her broken leg suspended in its splint and its bandages seemed to confirm the imminence of further evil.

"I cannot agree with you. They are my own flesh and blood."

Blushing violently, Jenny said, "Maybe I am the one to leave."

"You?" Mrs. Prickett sounded outraged. "You are my nurse. I couldn't get along without you. Besides, you are innocent of any wrongdoing. Isn't she, Mrs. Bowling?"

With her sense of justice appealed to, Gan could say only one thing. "Of course she is. Don't even think of such a thing, Jenny, dear."

Laurel squeezed Gan's arm excitedly, longing to tell her that Jenny was right, that she ought to go.

Mrs. Prickett laid down her ultimatum. "Talk it over with them tonight, Mrs. Bowling. By tomorrow morning, I want either Walter or Rome to leave this house."

Gan said quietly, "I am afraid you are over-stepping yourself, Mrs. Prickett." She turned and went out.

There was a tense silence in the room. Laurel could hear the jar flies loud in the locust trees. Sudden cries rose from Roy and Chris, who were arguing over a croquet game. Jenny picked up a palm leaf fan and began fanning Mrs. Prickett, whose face was red and perspiring.

"Just the same," Mrs. Prickett said as though to herself,

"something must be done."

Laurel tried to reassure herself, tried to believe that there was nothing Mrs. Prickett could do. The very effort increased her doubt. She became certain that Mrs. Prickett would do something. What, it was impossible to guess.

At supper Uncle Walter spoke to Rome only when he served the ham and deviled eggs. He had a swollen lip and Rome a bruised jaw to show for the fight, but inquiries from Roy were quickly stifled. Uncle Cam flicked them with a knowing blue eye and contented himself with winking at Laurel. Gan, presiding over the pitchers of iced tea and buttermilk at the head of the table, was grave and preoccupied. Only Jenny, who could always talk, chattered nervously about everything from the August drought that seemed to be setting in, to what Mr. and Mrs. Carlton were doing in Europe.

Gan seized on the latter subject and said that she would read them all a letter that had just arrived from Switzerland. Later, in the hall, Gan put on her glasses and took the letter out of her apron pocket. It was from Mother, Laurel knew in advance. If he could, Papa always avoided writing letters.

Gan started reading:

"How nice that you are all gathered there together, enjoying Blue Ridge View in the summer. I look forward to meeting Walter's sweetheart, Jenny. What a lovely name that is! And I know Rome will have some beautiful pictures to show us."

Edgar said darkly, "They ought to hear what's really going on."

"Dear," Gan said, "please don't interrupt me." She continued:

"At last we are in beautiful Switzerland, which is far more wonderful even than my geography book used to say. Beneath the high snowy peaks everything is so fresh and green.

144

And such wild flowers! They almost hurt your eyes. Butter-cups, daisies, bluebells, forget-me-nots. And the waterfalls, thousands of them, dashing down cold and clear from the glaciers. John keeps a pocket full of Swiss chocolate and munches it at all hours.

"Tomorrow our party will take the cable car up to see a glacier at close range. John is always making jokes about being the only man in a party of eight women. He says he feels like a Maharajah traveling with his harem."

Gan finished the letter with a sigh of satisfaction. "Well, well, they are having the time of their lives. Margaret has dreamed since she was a little girl of going to Europe. I'm glad now that she took her little inheritance to use for this trip."

"What'd they do if they heard about the battle of the millpond?" Edgar asked.

Gan looked at him over the tops of her glasses. "You know very well if they became worried over things here, they would leave the tour and come home. It would be a sin and a shame."

For a little while, there was silence in the hall. Through the open door, Laurel heard the alert clearing of Mrs. Prickett's throat.

Edgar shrugged and hunched himself down in his chair. His eyes went from Uncle Walter's puffed lip to Rome's bruised cheek. Laurel wondered what he was thinking. She assumed he was fairly neutral toward Uncle Walter, but she was not quite sure of his attitude toward Rome. Sometimes she thought he had a sort of admiration for his brother. But sometimes it seemed that he merely envied him. She was sure he resented the fact that Rome was not more definite about the promised trip to New York.

The next morning she was dusting the piano in the hall and elaborately ignoring Edgar, who was going over his list of calls for the day. Jenny came out of Mrs. Prickett's room and said, "Edgar, she wants to see you."

Mumbling to himself, he went in.

"Good morning, Edgar," Mrs. Prickett began. "Will you please shut the doors?"

With a parting smirk at Laurel, he closed the door into the hall. She stood motionless, clutching the dust cloth. A consultation between those two could mean no good. She felt a terrible compulsion to know what they were saying. She crept to the door on tiptoe, but the walls were too thick, the door too solid, for her to hear anything beyond the muffled sound of their voices.

Finally, as he came striding out, she hastened to occupy herself with straightening the desk.

"Aren't you through messing around here yet?" he wanted to know.

"Almost." She ran the dust cloth under the blotter, on which he had left his list. As he leaned forward, she saw in his shirt pocket a folded sheet of the lined tablet paper on which Mrs. Prickett wrote to her son. Also, there were some dollar bills. That was odd. If Mrs. Prickett had given him a memorandum to be filled, the money was unnecessary. Papa ran an account at Odlum and Blount's, and settled once a year when the tenants paid him his fourth of the tobacco money. If it had been just an item or two such as they got at the small store in Forest Mill, she had plainly given him too much money. No, it wasn't a memorandum, it was something else.

She asked with pretended carelessness. "Is Mrs. Prickett buying *Titanic* books for all her folks?"

He clutched at his pocket. "Get away from here and stop spying."

"Spying? What's there to spy about?"

"You needn't act so innocent. Bet you were listening at the door." He scowled at her, but the scowl didn't hide the question in his eyes.

"What if I did?"

"If you blab, you'll be sorry."

After he had gone, she saw that he had left his prospectus behind. That meant he didn't plan to canvass. She ran to the front porch. Already he was halfway down the walk to the yard gate. He walked fast across the lawn to the stable and soon reappeared riding Byron. Reaching the road, he turned left toward Cool Hill and Pigeon Run. Then she remembered his saying the night before that he was going to Forest Mill this morning to deliver some books. He must have changed his plans in order to do something for Mrs. Prickett. But what?

As she went back inside, she heard Gan say to Mrs. Prickett, "Are you through with the itinerary? I must answer Margaret's letter today, and I want to get her next address."

Itinerary? Laurel stood motionless. What was Mrs. Prickett doing with the itinerary? Had she written a letter herself? Then she must have carried out her threat. She must have told them.

Urgency swept her. She had to talk to somebody. This was something she could not handle alone. Reluctant to worry Gan, she went to look for Uncle Walter. She found him out at the woodpile arranging with one of the tenants to haul in the winter's supply of wood. Pausing at the gate, she called to him.

He glanced over his shoulder. "Be there in a minute."

It seemed an eternity until the man had gone, until Uncle Walter met her at the woodshed. "What now?" he asked.

She told him, begging him to overtake Edgar and find out what Mrs. Prickett was up to.

He eyed her dubiously. "Uh-huh. Trying to stick your nose into something else that's none of your business. What you need is more work to do."

"Oh, please, Uncle Walter, find out. It would be awful to break up their trip. They haven't even gotten to Italy yet. And then Mother wants to see Spain, she's always wanted to see Spain."

"You're crazy. I reckon Mrs. Prickett just wanted something from the store."

"Oh, it wasn't that, I know it wasn't that."

"You don't know any such thing. Run along and let me alone."

She knew then what she had to do, what she had wanted to avoid if possible. She came upon Rome reading in the hammock, and hesitated, gazing at the purple marks on his jaw, at the closed look on his face. "Rome," she began, fearing that he might hear the beating of her heart, "I—I have something to tell you."

At first she thought he was going to be as indifferent as Uncle Walter, but she was wrong. He sat up, snapped his book shut without marking the place. "It couldn't have been a letter," he said, "or she would have put it in an envelope."

Why hadn't she thought of that?

He went on hurriedly, "You say she gave him some bills, too? I have it, Laurel. She's sending them a cablegram. God knows what she's said."

She gasped. Such a thing had not occurred to her. As far as she knew, no one in the family had ever sent a cablegram.

"Come on." Rome was striding across the yard. "We'll make better time if we hitch both horses to the buggy."

WE. Even in the excitement, she felt the impact of the "we."

Appearing to sense the urgency in the air, Billy set about the harnessing without too much objection. Within ten minutes she and Rome were driving up the road at a fast trot. "When we catch up with him—if we do—pretend to be calm and casual," he warned her. "Edgar can be as stubborn as the devil."

"As if I didn't know," she blurted out.

He gave a short laugh.

They passed Cool Hill and Mr. Giffin's house. On the straight stretch of road ahead of them they saw Edgar riding at a leisurely canter. Rome urged Juno and Lady on with a

148

slap of the lines. The buggy wheels spun over the hard packed clay. Intent as she was on their mission, she was acutely conscious of Rome, of his nearness. How wonderful if they could ride on like this forever.

As they approached Edgar, he swung around in his saddle. There was the sudden opening of his face that expressed surprise. Then it became shut and dark.

They drew abreast. Rome waved. "Hello, there, what's your hurry?"

"Who said I was in a hurry? Looks like you're in a rush yourself.

Laurel saw Edgar's glance whip over her.

"Well, I did want to talk to you about that cablegram." Rome's voice was beautifully calm.

Edgar jumped as though Rome had thrown a stone at him. "What cablegram?"

"Don't worry. I know all about it."

"Snooper!" Edgar shot at her.

"Mrs. Prickett is an ill woman," Rome went on. "She magnifies things. I'm sure you don't want to upset John and Margaret's trip, do you?"

Looking glum, Edgar allowed Byron to slow down to a walk. Rome quietly pulled up the team to match his pace. Suddenly Edgar's eyes flashed at his brother. "It's all your fault," he accused.

Rome's lips tightened, but his tone was still placating. "I don't know what you're talking about. If Walter got excited over the picture, I couldn't help it. Who'd expect him to be so touchy?"

"You've been fooling around his girl. It wasn't only the picture. Reckon he's got eyes in his head."

"And you've got brains in yours. Would I be trying to break up Walter's engagement?"

"You darn near broke up Devoe's marriage."

"Don't be ridiculous." Rome spoke sharply.

"Want me to come right out and say what I know?"

149

"I don't want to hear any silly accusations, if that's what you mean."

Edgar's lips curled. "Didn't think you'd want me to say it."

The brothers glared at each other.

"If they find me irresistible—" Rome began, and stopped himself. "Listen, Edgar, we're getting off the subject. Considering all Margaret and John have done for you, you'd be damned ungrateful to spoil their tour."

Edgar winced. "They'd want to know what's going on."

"Nothing's going on. Jenny's out of the picture, and that's that."

Edgar looked unconvinced.

There was the sound of approaching wheels, and they turned out to let Mr. Giffin's surrey pass. As usual, he rode alone in the front seat, Mrs. Giffin alone in the back. Their size made this arrangement expedient. Rome lifted his hat, Laurel waved, and Edgar, who was bareheaded, merely nodded.

Rome resumed as though there had been no interruption, "After all, Mrs. Prickett is an outsider, she's not one of the family. You're not going to let her butt in and tell you what to do."

This thrust appeared to get through Edgar's guard. "How do I know you're not going to start something else?" he demanded.

"All I want is to be left in peace to paint. I have a show coming up in the fall, remember."

Laurel saw that Edgar had still not surrendered. Rome evidently saw it, too. "Suppose I promise there won't be any more trouble?" he said.

Oddly enough, Edgar's ire appeared to be stirred up afresh. "What's a promise to you?"

Instantly, she knew what was on Edgar's mind. He was thinking about Rome's unkept promise of a trip to New York. From his expression she judged that this was also occurring to Rome. After a moment's silence, he said gravely,

150

"To me a promise is something to be fulfilled, like the one I made to you. How would you like to go to New York with me in September?"

The sullen dark look vanished from Edgar's face. "Sure enough? You mean it?"

"As Laurel is my witness." Rome turned to give her a smile.

It was obvious that Edgar now had the problem of saving face. "If I don't send that cablegram, Old Lady Prickett will just get somebody else to do it."

"As I pointed out a few minutes ago," Rome answered, "you have brains. Does she have to know you haven't sent it?"

"I reckon not," Edgar conceded. "I could just give her back the money when she leaves."

chapter
16

LAUREL HAD no way of knowing what Edgar told or didn't tell Mrs. Prickett about the cablegram, but she looked so self-satisfied that she apparently believed it had been sent. Doubtless waiting for results, she continued knitting a sweater for Chris. She had also promised to make sweaters for Roy and Laurel.

"She's so conscientious," Gan said, "she feels she has fallen down on her job."

"Well, hasn't she?" Laurel asked, remembering the scene in the pantry.

"Shame," Gan scolded, but she could not keep the twinkle out of her eyes.

It was evident that Gan knew nothing of the cablegram. Uncle Walter had dismissed the idea so positively that Laurel hoped he had forgotten what she had said to him in the woodshed. Yet there was some danger of his asking a question or making a remark. She had to confess to Rome that she had been to Uncle Walter first about the matter. As she had anticipated, he looked displeased. He and Uncle Walter were on terms of the barest and most frigid politeness and did not speak to each other at all unless it was unavoidable.

"He has a suspicious nature," Rome muttered. "Better make sure he keeps his mouth shut."

She answered without thinking, "He isn't suspicious unless he has some reason." At the import of her own words, she blushed.

He looked at her oddly. "Just what do you mean by that?"

"He—he did have a reason," she said faintly.

"You, too, Laurel?"

She was silent.

He clasped her chin, tilted her face up toward his. She wanted to turn away and could not. Under the warm touch of his hand, her flesh tingled. Unwillingly, her eyes locked with his.

"Little Laurel," he said gently, "my sweet little Laurel."

What he might have said next she never knew. Edgar came through the archway in the lilac hedge and into the triangle of young locusts where they were standing. If he noticed anything unusual, he pretended not to. "Don't know how long we can stall off Old Lady Prickett," he said. "She figures on an answer soon."

Rome moved away from Laurel. "Well, it's just the first week in August, and they're not scheduled to sail back till the end of September. We've got to stall her. If she finds out she's been fooled, she'll make sure next time."

"She sure will," Edgar muttered, "and she'll tell on me, too."

"Don't worry about that," Rome reassured him.

153

"That's easy for you to say. Cousin John might be mad as heck with me. After all, maybe I ought to send that cable."

Laurel, who was gradually recovering from her moment of rapture, gave a little cry. "You can't, it would ruin everything."

Rome laid one arm carelessly across Edgar's shoulders. "You can't fool me, fellow, you're too smart to do anything like that. By the way, need any clothes for the trip? On second thought, it might be better to wait and get a new suit in New York. Something right in style."

Edgar's face changed, lighted as though against his will. For the time being, she felt, he wouldn't do anything. But you never could tell about Edgar. Often she fancied she could see thoughts moving in his eyes like shadowy things in dark water. She never could tell quite what they were. Maybe he would keep quiet for a while, but who could be sure how long?

In an inner ruthlessness of which she was sometimes capable, she asked herself why she cared so much. It was true she didn't want to spoil Papa and Mother's trip, but that wasn't all. She had the terrible fear that Rome might be blamed, that he might leave.

At supper that evening her fear was intensified. Uncle Walter said unexpectedly, "Laurel, I hope you got that nonsense out of your head about Mrs. Prickett."

At first she was too stunned to answer. Then she realized that if she didn't say something quickly he might come right out and mention what she had said to him about the cable. "Papa always says I get my imagination from reading too many novels," she spluttered. "Will you please find a gizzard for me, Uncle Walter, that's my favorite piece of chicken." She held out her plate.

Automatically, he began turning over the pieces of fried chicken with the big silver spoon. "What you need is more work to do," he remarked as he had before.

Uncle Cam put down his knife, on which he had been

conveying some potato salad to his mouth. "She does plenty. Her grandmother, my sister Anna, never even had to make her own bed."

Laurel could have kissed Uncle Cam. That was just the thing to start an argument with Uncle Walter, who thought of work as the world's panacea.

Jenny, who had been subdued since the fight, joined in, evidently glad of a chance to support Uncle Walter. She told in detail how much work her mother did, how much work her brothers and sisters did, how much work she herself did. Then she dwelt at length on her father, who, besides running his farm, was a county road supervisor and a member of the school board. Laurel watched Uncle Walter's face. Though he must have heard all this before, he still wore a look of satisfaction and approval. Perhaps he was on the way to forgiving Jenny for the trouble she had caused him.

As to how Jenny herself felt, Laurel still had her doubts. Plainly, she was not ready to break up with Uncle Walter. At the same time, her head was at least halfway turned by the charms of Rome.

In their room that night, Laurel asked her, "Is Uncle Walter still mad with you?"

"Some, I reckon." She added as she brushed her hair, "It was lucky you took a notion to jump in that pond when you did. Never will know how you got up the nerve. Ugh! that old black water. Gives me the creeps just to think about it."

"Oh, it was nothing." Inwardly she still quaked at the way the water had looked. She didn't quite know herself how she had summoned up the courage to do what she had done.

Jenny went on half to herself, "Walter's a fine man, the kind a girl can depend on, but his mind is always running on work and business, never says anything fancy."

"Like Rome?" Laurel asked.

Jenny shrugged.

"And Uncle Walter is plain looking, isn't he?"

"Oh, he looks all right. Wish he'd comb his hair more, it's

155

always sticking up."

Not at all satisfied about the situation, Laurel could not help pursuing the matter. "You—you'd rather have Rome, wouldn't you?"

"Laurel, for heaven's sake, how you do talk. Since I'm engaged to Walter and Rome is his relative, of course I have to get along with him, too." She began braiding her hair for the night. "Don't see why Walter didn't want me to be in that picture. It would be nice. Wouldn't it be funny to have all the Vanderbilts and people like that looking at me?"

"What difference would it make?" Laurel asked, thinking in her heart that she wouldn't mind that herself, particularly if it were Rome's picture.

"You think I'd look all right in that picture?" Jenny inquired wistfully.

"Sure. Why not? But I reckon you won't have much to do with Rome after this, will you?"

"What do you mean by that? All I've been is friendly. Maybe I'll be a little less friendly. More, just polite."

What about Rome? Laurel asked herself. Would he really leave Jenny alone now? The question was torture. The fact that she couldn't answer it, that it hung over her unanswered, left her in a state of mute misery. The memory of the way he had spoken in the locust triangle, of the way he had clasped her chin in his hand, did not lessen her uneasiness. It served only to tantalize her, to make her dream more sharply a dream that reason told her could never be realized.

Since the day of the fight, Rome had not returned to the millpond. The unfinished picture stood against the wall in his room, and nobody spoke of it. Whenever Laurel went there to make up his bed, she looked at it with varied emotions. While she felt a certain sadness that it was not completed, she had a guilty satisfaction that Jenny was not in it. Justifying this satisfaction, she told herself that anyway a person didn't have to be in every painting. Just the pond and the trees would be enough. But she did not tell Rome this.

She felt shyer than ever about speaking to him now, avoided being alone with him. Not because she didn't long for that, but because something restrained her.

Meantime, Rome seemed restless. He lounged in the triangle with a book of poems or played croquet with Chris and Roy. Sometimes he took them swimming, leaving Uncle Cam free to enjoy a long siesta. At least once a day Rome would go in for a little visit with Mrs. Prickett. He would read to her or ask about her son, or listen with his head slightly on one side as she told about the many virtues and achievements of the late Mr. Prickett.

"Lawsy," Brindy said to Laurel one day, "Mr. Rome sure is sweetening her up."

"He's not either. He's just being nice to her because she's sick."

"Uh-huh." Brindy surveyed her through squinted eyes.

Laurel squirmed.

"Yes, sir," Brindy continued, "that's one sweet-talking man."

"It's a good thing," Laurel retorted defensively. "You certainly never hear Uncle Walter or Edgar say anything sweet."

"Reckon not. All's the matter with Edgar, he hasn't got used to himself yet. And maybe Mr. Walter don't talk sweet, but he talks straight. You always know where *he* stands."

The floor undulated, and Gan came in from the back porch through the little kitchen. "Brindy," she said, "I noticed at breakfast that the silver was getting a little dark. Set it all here on the table, and I'll clean it while you fix the vegetables."

"Yessum, Miss Celia, that'll be a big help."

Before Gan could think of a new task for her, Laurel oozed softly out of the kitchen and into the darkened dining room. She was thinking about what Brindy had said. But already she had found a reason for Rome's kindness to Mrs. Prickett. Of course. If and when Mrs. Prickett found out that

157

the cable had not been sent, he wanted to be in a position to use persuasion.

She knew that Uncle Walter, too, had been viewing Rome with an increasingly critical eye. Naturally, he couldn't ask him why he didn't keep on with the picture of the millpond.. But that day at dinner he brought up something different. Turning to Rome, he said bluntly, "Billy has lumbago, and the stable needs cleaning out. How about manning a pitchfork this afternoon?"

Except for a little flare-up in his eyes, Rome's expression did not change. "Can't think of a more delightful occupation for a summer afternoon, but I told Mrs. Prickett I'd get something for her at Forest Mill."

"Might have known you'd have some excuse."

"Then," said Rome coolly, "why did you ask me?"

They glared at each other in silence.

Gan said, "Walter, dear, will you see if anyone will have ham?"

Jenny, who had been watching anxiously, burst out, "This is the best ham. Do you have a special secret for curing it?"

"I think maybe John does have a secret," Gan answered. "I know he smokes it for six weeks with hickory wood, and has it rubbed first with black pepper and molasses, as well as salt. And of course he doesn't think a ham should be eaten until it's two years old."

"My pa certainly would say he was right," Jenny concurred and launched into a description of their smokehouse, which was brick instead of frame like the one at Blue Ridge View.

Laurel was thinking of hog-killing time, which usually came after the first heavy frost in November. She and Chris and Roy were not allowed to watch, and the proceedings were regarded with fascination and terror. A fire was built near the woodpile, and from the kitchen window you could see the roaring red pillar of flame. The fire heated the water in the great black cauldron, where the hogs were dipped and the hair scalded off. Then the nude bodies were suspended in a row on a pole supported by two tall forked sticks. But what she remembered most vividly was the wild desperate squeals of the hogs when Booker cut their throats.

She was startled back to the present. Someone had called her name. "Where were you?" Rome asked, smiling. "Would you like to drive over to Forest Mill? I'll get you some candy."

A sudden convulsive pain shot through her. Candy! As though she were five instead of fifteen.

"Can I go?" Roy cried.

"Me, too," Chris chimed in. "Can I go, too?"

" '*May* I go,' " Gan said severely. "I suppose you may if Rome has no objections."

"Fine," Rome said.

Laurel imagined herself announcing with dignity that she was busy, that she could not possibly go. At the same time, she knew that she would do no such thing. Even if she were being treated as a child, she still had to go. When they started off, however, her feelings were somewhat soothed. Chris and Roy themselves decided that they would sit on the floor in the back of the buggy, as they did when they went out with Papa and Mother. Thus she alone shared the seat with Rome. She sat close to her side, leaving a space between them, and stared straight ahead.

"Why do you sit so far away?" Rome asked. "Are you afraid of me?"

She did not answer.

chapter
17

THE NEXT letter from Mother came from the Grand Palace
Hotel, Lake Lugano, in Italy. It went on in Mother's usual
vein about the beauty of the lake from their hotel window,
the little white steamer, the mountain beyond. Gan read it
aloud in the hall that evening.

Before the first paragraph was finished, Mrs. Prickett
called out through her open door, "Mrs. Bowling, what is the
date of that letter?"

Gan told her, a faint reproof in her voice at the interruption.

Laurel stiffened, turned uneasily toward Rome. He gave a
scarcely perceptible shake of the head. She looked at Edgar.

He flushed, raked his feet up under his chair, and stared back in a frank betrayal of concern.

As Gan read on, Laurel could hear only the silence in the next room. Any minute Mrs. Prickett would call for Edgar, and the storm would break. The letter ended saying they looked forward to moving on to Venice, then Florence, and Rome.

Mrs. Prickett did not call for Edgar until the next morning, which was Sunday. She had evidently chosen the time when they would be getting ready for church. As Laurel started upstairs to her room, she saw him go in, then heard both doors close. She tried to listen while Jenny conducted a monologue on what dress to wear, but she could hear nothing.

At midday, when they were going in to dinner, she heard Edgar whisper to Rome, "She's mad as the devil. Says she's going to get that cable off if it's the last thing she does."

How? Laurel wondered.

Meantime, Uncle Walter was talking about the horses, which he had turned out to graze the lawn when they came back from church. He was saying to Uncle Cam, "I put your old Jezebel out there, too. She was kicking her stall."

Uncle Cam shook his head. "Better keep an eye on her. She's not very sociable."

"Oh, she's too busy eating grass to get in trouble."

"Maybe so." Uncle Cam did not look convinced.

When the ice cream came, Chris finished his quickly, then slipped away from the table while Gan was talking to Jenny. Laurel saw him snatch up his butterfly net from the hall floor and disappear. When Gan turned and noted his absence, she said, "Christopher did not ask to be excused. Where is he?"

"Oh," Roy told her, "he's after a yellow butterfly he saw before dinner."

"Butterfly or no butterfly, he knows better than to leave the table like that."

161

"We're all about done," Uncle Cam said placatingly.

While they continued in the slow enjoyment of their ice cream, Jenny launched into an account of how she had been disciplined as a child.

Suddenly there was a high, angry squeal from the direction of the front lawn. "The horses!" Uncle Walter sprang up and rushed out. On a single impulse the others followed him to the front porch. As he ran through the yard gate, Laurel looked beyond. Lady and Juno, as well as Byron, were grazing peacefully near the corn-house. Then she saw that Jezebel was loping away from the left-hand corner of the lawn with her ears backed. There was no time to think or wonder. Uncle Walter was bending over something near the horseblock.

"Chris!" As she ran forward, Laurel saw the blood, the fresh scarlet blood on his forehead and face. Nearby lay the butterfly net. Uncle Walter took his clean Sunday handkerchief out of his pocket and gently wiped the blood off Chris's face. Then she saw where Chris's forehead was laid open and turned her head away with a feeling of such illness as she had never known in her life. When she looked again, Uncle Walter was running his hands over Chris's arms and legs. The others were there now, surrounding them. He looked up at Gan. "No broken bones, but—" He nodded toward the wound, which was still bleeding.

"Try to staunch the blood," Gan said, pulling off her little white apron and handing it to him. "We must get him to the house."

As Uncle Walter lifted Chris in his arms, she turned to Edgar. "Dear, ride up to Mr. Giffin's and telephone for Dr. Walton. If he isn't at home, find out where he is and go after him."

Edgar darted off to catch Byron.

Chris had not spoken, had not even moaned. His eyes were closed. In an agony of fear, Laurel walked close behind Uncle Walter. Suppose Chris never spoke again. Suppose—

162

the supposition was too awful. She fought it back, refused to face it. Roy was walking beside her, carrying the butterfly net. The impish look was gone from his face, and he was as white as his shirt collar. He must be sharing her fear. Without a word, she gave him a little hug. They walked on. The others followed in a quiet procession.

On the red brick walk the drops of blood were scarcely noticeable, but they made a scarlet trail up the porch steps. Uncle Walter asked Roy to open the doors as he passed through the hall, along the back porch, and into Gan's room, where he laid Chris on the white expanse of Gan's fourposter. She had gone ahead to spread a clean sheet over the bed and to lay out heavy turkish towels.

Laurel grew conscious of the insistent tinkling of Mrs. Prickett's bell. Gan turned to her. "Please see what Mrs. Prickett wants. Jenny, you stay here and help me. We must stop the bleeding."

In a daze, Laurel reached Mrs. Prickett's bedside. Mrs. Prickett put down the bell. "What has happened?"

Laurel found that at first she couldn't speak at all. Finally, speech came, stiff and jumbled. The thing seemed even worse when put into words.

Mrs. Prickett turned deathly white. "Call Walter here at once."

Uncle Walter strode in, red-faced and tousled, his eyes squinted with worry. Laurel waited just outside the open door.

Mrs. Prickett burst out, "We must cable the Carltons immediately."

"What good will that do? If he dies, he'll be dead and buried before they can get here."

"He's not going to die!" Laurel cried. It was not a hope, it was a protest, a protest against all the things in life that were too dreadful to be borne.

Uncle Walter turned on her. "Shut up. We've got enough on our hands without you carrying on."

163

His roughness was a help, a sort of counterirritant.

She went toward Uncle Cam, who was pacing up and down the hall, twisting at his beard. "Plague on it," he muttered, "it's all my fault. Weaver told me that horse was mean. Didn't think he knew what he was talking about. Been living too high since she got here, that's the trouble."

Rome appeared at the front door. "Edgar's gone. If Dr. Walton is at home, it won't take him long to get here in his machine."

"What if he's not at home?" Her question was a plea for reassurance.

Evidently returning from Gan's room, Brindy passed slowly across the back porch, her head bent. It was like a sign, Laurel thought desperately, and gave a little choking gasp.

Rome put a comforting arm about her shoulders. Any other time she would have been thrilled beyond expression. Not now. Not when Chris might be dying. She wished only that Rome were Papa, that Papa's arm were about her.

For the first time that she could remember, she was experiencing the tortures of remorse. She hadn't been very nice to Chris this summer. More than once he'd asked her to go butterfly hunting and she had refused. He'd begged her to tell him a witch tale, and she'd asked him not to bother her. She could see his serious blue eyes, hear him say, "What's the matter with you, Laurel, you're not like you used to be?" If she'd only been nice to him, if she only had. Now she might never have the chance, never again. Too choked up to speak, she moved away from Rome.

In half an hour, Edgar came back. Dr. Walton was not at home. Mrs. Walton had said he was visiting Stud Paxton over on Branch Road north of Blue Ridge View. Branch Road swept in an irregular semicircle from Tyler Morgan's blacksmith's shop northwest past the Paxton place, and ended finally at Forest Mill. From the Paxtons' the doctor was going on to Job Crawley's. Neither family had a telephone.

Edgar's plan was to cut across Blue Ridge View plantation and try to catch him before he left the Paxtons'.

A moment later they heard Byron's hooves ringing on the rocks in the lane.

Still muttering to himself, Uncle Cam went out the front door. Then Laurel saw him bridling Jezebel. When he rode toward the big gate, Billy was running beside him, apparently protesting. Next Billy was standing with his back to the gate as though to bar the way. Finally, Uncle Cam won, the gate was opened; his old black hat went bobbing off between the hedgerows.

Already overcome by emotion, Laurel had seen all this with a certain detachment. It was like viewing something at a distance through glass, something that had no connection with you. Now she realized that Uncle Cam was a very old man, dreadfully upset, and that it was a murderously hot August afternoon. She herself should have tried to stop him. She ran down to Billy. "Oh, why didn't you make him stay here?" she wailed.

"You talk like I didn't try. Mr. Cam is set. Ain't often he gets set, but he's set now. Nothing short of hog-tying him would of stopped him."

"But what's the use?"

"Said he was going to Crawleys' case Edgar missed Doc at Paxtons'."

"I wish you had hog-tied him."

He shook his head. "Can't interfere with folks but so far. Blames hisself. Maybe he's better off going than setting here cussing hisself out."

"Maybe I could catch him on Juno."

"Wouldn't do any good." He added, "Fact is, not knowing what's going to be needed, we'd better keep the team handy."

Miserably, she returned to the house. Uncle Walter and Rome were sitting at opposite ends of the hall. She wondered transiently if they were still mad with each other, or if they just preferred not to talk. She found Roy sprawled on the

165

back porch, his face buried in Sir Julian's side, sniffling. Sir Julian was licking his cheek.

She tiptoed to Gan's door, peered through the screen. Chris lay still, his forehead covered with a bandage. Gan sat beside the bed fanning him with her palm leaf fan. Jenny stood by the window, for once silent. Gan glanced up. "You may come in, dear, if you'll be very quiet."

She went in, softly closing the screen door after her, and sat down on the footstool beside the cold fireplace. Chris looked so very white, so still. This was how death was, she thought, this stillness. It was a simple thing, a time when you stopped moving.

Gan stopped fanning to look at the little gold watch that was pinned with a fleur de lis on her Sunday black silk dress. On her forehead, which was usually so serene, there were wrinkles of concern. She snapped the watch shut and resumed the fanning. Laurel had never known the house to be so quiet. There were no voices, not even Jenny's. Mrs. Prickett's little bell was silent. Outside she could hear the jar flies in the locust trees, and from the poultry yard rose the occasional caw-cawing of a hen or the quacking of one of the Peking ducks. Time seemed to have stopped.

Suddenly Chris moaned. It was a beautiful sound, a sound of life. But he did not open his eyes. Again he was quiet. A small scarlet stain had appeared on the white bandage. Laurel looked away from it into the cold black depths of the fireplace. She did not know actually how long it was before Dr. Walton got there, she knew only that it seemed much longer than the span of her own life. Surprisingly soon after she heard his automobile, he was stepping purposefully along the back porch and into Gan's room.

"Oh," Gan said, keeping her voice low, "I am glad to see you."

He nodded. Already he was bending over Chris, taking his pulse. When this was done, he made no comment. He opened his bag and took out his stethoscope. Fitting the black tenta-

166

cles into his ears, he uncovered Chris's chest. Again he said nothing.

Gan, who had risen from her chair and moved back, whispered urgently, "It's the gash on his head that we are worried about."

He replaced the stethoscope in his bag, turned and lifted the bandage. Laurel, having sprung soundlessly to her feet, could see the gaping wound. She closed her eyes, felt that she was going to be sick.

The doctor said, "Please clear a table and move it up here."

Laurel was conscious of Gan's movements as she did this with Jenny's help. Then she felt Gan's hand on her shoulder, and opened her eyes. Dr. Walton had removed his coat, rolled up his shirt sleeves. Already the room was permeated with the unforgettable smell of iodoform. "Dear," Gan said, "please ask Brindy to bring the water I told her to boil."

Thankfully, Laurel escaped from the room. She gave the message to Brindy, not questioning her presence in the kitchen Sunday afternoon when she was supposed to be at home. Instead of going into the hall, she went to her retreat in the boxwoods. It was cool and peaceful in the green dusk. But the peace could not reach her today. She threw herself down on the rustic seat and began to sob.

chapter
18

THE SUPPER bell did not ring as usual that evening. Instead, Edgar came to call her. "Figured you'd be here," he said.

She sat up, mopping at her eyes with the hem of her dress. "How's Chris?"

"It took nine stitches. He came to while the doctor was doing it."

"Then it—it hurt him."

"Aunt Celia says he held still. Once he asked if the doctor was 'most through."

She wiped harder at her eyes.

"Come on," Edgar said, "no use to do that."

She followed him slowly into the dining room, not because

she was hungry, but because she couldn't stand to be alone any longer. Dr. Walton was there, too, looking serious and remote as he always did. As usual, the ends of his dark mustache drooped downward. Even here at the table, the scent of iodoform still clung to him.

Uncle Walter asked bluntly, "Is Chris going to get well?"

"I have done what I could."

"He wouldn't be conscious if the concussion were serious, would he?"

"A concussion is always serious. However, the boy is healthy."

Laurel had thought only of the gash. Now there was the concussion to think of—a vague and terrible thing that didn't happen to anybody you knew, certainly not your own brother. She sat in shocked silence.

"Dear," Gan said, "eat your chicken salad. Brindy has outdone herself."

"She certainly has," Jenny agreed. "I'm going to get her recipe and take it home. Mama always adds a few hickory nuts and some chopped green peppers, but this is wonderful. Don't you think so, Walter?" Without waiting for his answer, she launched into the whole matter of chicken salads, what kind of chickens to use, on what occasions chicken salad was best served, and what kind of bread should accompany it.

Glancing around, Laurel saw that it was a relief to everyone to let Jenny's busy tongue fend off the oppressive quiet.

In a brief lull while Jenny drank some iced tea, Gan said, "Did anybody call Mr. Cam?"

"Oh," Laurel cried, dismayed to find that she had forgotten him, "he's gone. He went to Job Crawley's, thinking Edgar might miss Dr. Walton at the Paxton place."

"When did he leave?"

"Right after Edgar left the second time."

"Oh, dear, even if he went all the way to the Paxtons', he's had time to be back."

Uncle Walter said with authority, "He has sense enough to take a rest and start home when it gets cooler."

Dr. Walton folded his napkin. "I have to call on Mrs. Crawley now, I'll tell him I've been here." He rose. "Thank you for the supper, Mrs. Bowling. I'll look at the boy before I go."

"And Mrs. Prickett wants to see you," Jenny reminded him.

He did not stay long with Chris, whom Brindy had been watching while they ate. When he went into Mrs. Prickett's room, Laurel heard her ask him to close the doors.

That was strange, she thought. Then she assumed that Mrs. Prickett was demanding to know the truth about Chris. Since he never committed himself, it wasn't surprising to hear the insistent murmur of Mrs. Prickett's voice for several minutes. At last he came hurriedly out and asked Laurel to call his driver from the kitchen, where Brindy had given him his supper. Shortly afterwards she heard the engine start and felt a surge of thankfulness that now Dr. Walton would find out about Uncle Cam.

Huddled on the front steps, she sat waiting for the sound of the doctor's automobile returning to Pigeon Run. It would be a sort of guarantee that Uncle Cam was all right. But the sound did not come. She became convinced that something was wrong. Going inside, she found Uncle Walter in the hall and begged him to hitch up the team and drive to the Crawleys'. He refused gruffly, telling her she was a silly child. He pointed out with sharp logic that Uncle Cam must have decided to spend the night. If he had gotten sick, wasn't the doctor there?

Rome had come down from his room in time to hear this. Ignoring Uncle Walter, he said to her, "You're right, Laurel, something may have happened to him. I'll hitch up and go with you."

"Don't be a fool," Uncle Walter growled as he had done on another occasion. He stood up menacingly.

Rome said coolly, "This is no time to forget yourself, Walter. When Aunt Celia comes out of Chris's room, tell her where we've gone."

Billy had gone home sometime before, but Rome showed himself quite capable of hitching the team to the buggy. With two horses they could make better time.

Though the night was sultry, the darkness made it seem much cooler than the day had been. As they crossed the bridge at a smart trot, the clatter of the horses' hooves mingled with the rushing of the water over the rocks below. After the inactivity, the waiting, the sound and motion were a release.

Her thoughts turned to Rome driving there beside her in the night. Rome had listened to her. Rome cared about Uncle Cam.

At the church on the hill overlooking Forest Mill, she directed him to turn right. It was only three miles now to the Crawleys'. They had met no one, so it was evident that both Uncle Cam and the doctor were still there. They drove alternately through woods and open fields, palely outlined in the starlight.

"You like the country?" Rome asked.

Like the country? The question was so startling that for a moment she couldn't answer. With all her questioning, she had never asked herself that. She caught a whiff from the woods, a whiff of old leaves lying under the trees, of living leaves on the branches. It was a woodsy smell, a smell she had always known and liked without realizing it.

"Of course I like it," she said.

"Aren't you curious about the city, about New York for instance?"

"I'd like to go there; I love to go to Lynchburg." She thought of the steep cobbled street leading down to Union Station, of the clanging hooves of the dray horses. She recalled the odor of over-ripe bananas at a fruit stand, blended with the scent of roasting coffee and coal smoke. Then on

171

Main Street there was the ten-cent store, and the fancy grocer's, where Mother bought celery and cranberries for Thanksgiving.

"Lynchburg," he said, "can't hold a candle to New York. Someday I'd like to show it to you."

Her heart gave a little jump. To see New York with Rome! It was beyond imagining. "That—that would be wonderful."

"Not too wonderful for you."

Ahead, up a lane to the left, she saw the lights of the Crawley house. "You turn there," she told him, and once more concern for Uncle Cam crowded out other thoughts.

There was no sign of Uncle Cam's horse, but Dr. Walton's driver sat in the Ford runabout at the gate. Uncle Cam had heat prostration, he said. The doctor had given him some medicine, and he was now asleep. In an aside to Rome, she heard him add that Mrs. Crawley was in labor.

Mr. Crawley came to the door and invited them into the parlor. He was a bald little man in shirt sleeves and red galluses. His eyes were bloodshot, and his mustache constantly twitched. "Don't you worry, Miss Laurel," he said, "the old man's resting quiet. Doc says he'll be all right tomorrow. You all set down."

From somewhere in the house rose a scream. He turned and ran out.

Laurel sat down in a mission rocker and looked at a large portrait of Mr. and Mrs. Crawley over the mantelpiece. It was a wedding portrait. She sat very straight with her voluminous white dress billowing about her, her veil drooping over her forehead. Very slicked down and solemn, he stood back of her, one hand on her shoulder, the other held primly to his breast. The recurrent screams, she thought, did not go with the picture.

Rome was moving restlessly about the room, glancing from the what-not filled with sea shells and knickknacks to a large Bible resting on a table in the center of the room. A red

172

fringed cover adorned the table, hung almost to the rose-patterned carpet.

"We'll go," he said, "as soon as we see the doctor."

"And Uncle Cam," she added.

Her eyes fell on the doctor's coat hung on a straight chair near the door. A piece of familiar-looking paper protruded from one of the pockets. She took another look. It was like the red-lined paper in Mrs. Prickett's tablet, the paper on which she had written the cablegram to Papa and Mother. "Look!" she cried, snatching it out.

They read it together. Another cablegram.

"Nice message," Rome muttered. "The news about Chris tops the rest. We'll have to show it to Aunt Celia."

"I hate to worry Gan any more than she's worried already."

"So do I," he answered with real sincerity. "But there's nothing else to do. We can't hope to intercept it a third time."

Mr. Crawley came back and showed them up to the guest room, where Uncle Cam was sleeping peacefully under what was probably Mrs. Crawley's best crocheted counterpane. "Leave him be," Mr. Crawley said, "he'll more'n likely be able to ride home tomorrow."

"Thank you," Laurel told him as they went downstairs. "I—I hope Mrs. Crawley will be all right."

"I reckon it will be according to God's will. She's getting along in years to have the first one."

They drove home slowly, wrapped in the still sultriness of the summer night. Laurel felt drowsiness creeping over her, pinched herself to stay awake. The wheels turned rhythmically, the horses' hooves beat a monotonous tattoo on the hard road. She fell into a doze, roused herself, then lapsed once more into the pleasant abyss of sleep.

She woke to the echoing clatter they made on the covered bridge. She was leaning against Rome, his arm was about her. "It's all right, sweet," he said gently, and kissed her.

chapter
19

WHEN LAUREL heard Dr. Walton's automobile the following morning, she tensed, stood waiting uneasily in the center of the hall. Had he discovered the loss of the cablegram? Gan had not yet been told about it, and she was now in Chris's room.

Rome came running downstairs, obviously with the same thought in mind. For an instant they faced each other in silence. There was remembrance in his eyes, and something else. She looked away.

He said quickly, "We don't have time to tell Aunt Celia now. We'll have to wait and see if he's missed the paper."

They stayed there while Dr. Walton went into Chris's

room and came out again, accompanied by Gan. "What do you think?" Gan asked him.

He cocked his head on one side and looked down. "We'll have to wait and see, Mrs. Bowling."

Jenny opened Mrs. Prickett's door. "Doctor, Mrs. Prickett wants to see you." She went across to the dining room with a tray.

Laurel saw his hand go to his side pocket, explore it briefly. He shook his head, and went in.

"Aunt Celia," Rome said, "I think you'd better go in there, too." He took her arm and propelled her through the door. Laurel followed.

"Have you sent it?" Mrs. Prickett was demanding.

"No. Haven't been back to Pigeon Run."

Mrs. Prickett turned to glare at Gan and Rome. "If you please, I want to talk to the doctor in private."

Dr. Walton waved his hand. "It's all right. Mrs. Bowling may want to add something to the cablegram."

"Cablegram?" Gan's bewilderment was unmistakable.

It was Dr. Walton's turn to look bewildered. "The cablegram to Mr. and Mrs. Carlton. Hadn't you discussed it with Mrs. Prickett?"

"Discussed it? I knew nothing about it." Gan's gaze was fixed on Mrs. Prickett.

Mrs. Prickett said defiantly: "You were occupied with Christopher. I had to take matters into my own hands."

"What did you say in that message?"

"The truth about what's going on here. Suppose Chris dies, or someone commits murder." She glanced significantly at Rome.

Gan seemed to rise inches beyond her normal height. Her eyes flamed. When she spoke, her voice was lower than usual, the result no doubt of a monumental self-control. "You dared do that without consulting me?"

"I dare do what is right."

"And you judge that for me, for this whole family? Let me

175

tell you, Mrs. Prickett, you have overstepped your authority again, and I will not have it. I will not have you sneaking messages out of this house."

Dr. Walton said sharply, "You deceived me, Mrs. Prickett." He took some bills from his wallet. "Here is the money you gave me for the cable."

It was odd, Laurel thought, how defiant Mrs. Prickett still managed to look. Even her stiffly suspended leg suggested a weapon. "Mr. and Mrs. Carlton would thank me," she snapped, "for telling them the truth."

Gan turned to Dr. Walton. "You understand what a blow such a message would be. They might cut short their trip."

"Quite so, Mrs. Bowling. I must leave now, I'll be back tomorrow."

Suddenly Mrs. Prickett's eyes focused on Laurel. "What is that child doing in here?"

"She is not a child," Rome said.

Laurel looked at him gratefully.

Mrs. Prickett scrutinized him. Was she wondering why, after his recent kindness, he was now opposing her? "Just what do you mean by that?" she asked.

"I mean," he answered quickly, "that she takes a more adult view of things than you realize. If it hadn't been for her, Edgar would have sent the first message."

Laurel wished he had not brought that up. But he evidently sensed as she did the direction in which Mrs. Prickett's thoughts were turning. He had taken a sure means of diverting her.

"So there was another attempt!" Gan exclaimed.

"Yes," Mrs. Prickett said. "You didn't seem to pay much attention to that fight between Rome and Walter at the millpond."

A change came over Gan's face. The indignation turned to sadness. "That was strictly a family affair. It is best forgotten."

"Do you think Rome and Walter have forgotten it? Here

176

they are under the same roof. Any time they may try again to kill each other."

"Don't be absurd, Mrs. Prickett. You lie here and imagine things."

"Imagine things indeed. Nobody's imagination could keep up with this household." She paused, then added grimly, "I warn you, Mrs. Bowling, there's worse to come."

"Nonsense." The floor vibrated eloquently as Gan went back through the passage to Chris.

Laurel and Rome were left gazing at Mrs. Prickett's flushed face. Ignoring Laurel, she said to him, "I reckon you'll be going back to New York soon."

"I have no idea of leaving," he said quietly, "until things here are in better shape."

Laurel followed him into the hall, genuinely shocked by what Mrs. Prickett had said. She had broken an unquestioned law of hospitality. Never in Laurel's life had she heard anyone suggest to a guest that he leave. Cousin Agatha had spent the whole of last summer with them. A school friend of Mother's had once stayed six months. The nearest Mother had come to any kind of protest was to exclaim one day, "Oh, dear me, I can't think of what to have for dinner. We've had everything over and over since Rose has been here." Any time Papa might arrive home from Lynchburg or Pigeon Run bringing a stranger. Whoever he was, he was given the Company Room and the breast of the chicken. These things were ritual. Now Mrs. Prickett had not only violated the code of Blue Ridge View, she had chosen to insult Rome.

In the hall Laurel's words tumbled over themselves. "Please don't mind what she said. She has no right. I'll tell Papa and Mother, they'll never have her here again."

He smiled. "I hope not. There's nothing worse than a conscientious busybody. But don't let it worry you, darling. Just consider the source. After all, she's not a member of the family."

177

"No, thank goodness!" Her exclamation was tempered by her delight over hearing him call her darling. Her happiness was like a soft haze overlying the dark area of her anxiety about Chris. It was strange, she thought, how things could exist in you side by side. If you could be all one way, at least at a time, life would be so much easier.

Glancing outside, she saw Billy opening the big gate for Uncle Cam. She rushed down to meet him at the horseblock. Jezebel looked somewhat chastened, and Uncle Cam was pale. "How's my boy?" he asked before dismounting.

"Tolerable, I reckon. You know Dr. Walton never tells you much."

"Uh-huh, I know that." He slid stiffly down from the saddle. "Reckon that's sensible, specially when you don't know."

Billy came to take Jezebel, and she held tight to Uncle Cam's arm as he went toward his house. "Feel a little poorly," he said, "think I'll lie down till dinnertime."

It was pleasantly cool inside, and she dropped into his rocker while he stretched out on the big four-poster with its red-and-white yarn counterpane.

"How's Mrs. Crawley?" she asked.

"Mighty proud. So's he. They've got a son at last. Named him Joseph."

She thought of the neat parlor, the cabinet full of bric-a-brac. Joseph would be toddling over to play with the sea shells, the vases. Maybe he would pull out the fringed red cloth from under the Bible on the center table, and bring the huge book down on his head. She could hear him wailing, see Mrs. Crawley running to pick him up. Needless to say, he would be spoiled. Even if they did spoil him, she was glad the Crawleys had a child.

Uncle Cam pulled thoughtfully at his whiskers. "So you came to see about your good-for-nothing old uncle?"

"Of course. Only don't talk like that about yourself."

"Cam's been a bad boy," he mumbled.

"I wish more people were bad the way you are."

He chuckled softly. "Now, now, that's my Laurel." He was silent for a little while, then went on in a different tone, "Reckon you know how much I think of you, child. Reckon that gives me the right to say something. Watch out for that Rome."

chapter

20

IT WAS two mornings later that Gan came out on the back porch, where Laurel was telling Roy a story. For the first time in days, Gan was smiling. "Laurel, you and Roy may come in to see Chris for a few minutes."

They found him propped up on two big pillows, with a fresh bandage around his head. He was white-faced and thin, and his blue eyes were more prominent than usual. He gazed back at them solemnly.

"Heh," Roy said.

"Heh," Chris responded in a weak voice.

"I caught that yellow butterfly for you," Roy said, "I've got him."

"How you know it's the same one?"

"It was still around the horseblock."

"Thanks."

Roy twisted at his belt. "Does it still hurt?"

"Feels kinda funny." Frowning, Chris ran his fingers over the bandage.

The air was still heavy with iodoform. Laurel had the feeling that the smell would stay with her all her life.

"What made you go so close to that old horse?" Roy inquired.

"I wasn't looking at the horse, I was looking at the butterfly."

"You know Uncle Cam always says to look where you're going."

"I was," Chris maintained.

Laurel had a compelling impulse to touch Chris, to do something for him. "Want me to read you a chapter in *The Last of the Mohicans?*" she asked.

"Tomorrow," he answered.

"Now," Gan said, "I think you all had better run along and let him rest."

Laurel left the room feeling as though she had been given a wonderful present.

Running to the kitchen, she announced to Brindy, "I want to make a chocolate cake for Chris. It's his favorite, you know. It'll be a surprise."

Brindy paused in her scrubbing of the kitchen table "It sure will." Her tone belied the irony in her words. "Better put some wood in the stove and get to work so you'll be out of the way of my dinner."

"Then what must I do?"

"Set out your things on the table here, then you won't miss nothing."

"Will you tell me the recipe?"

"I did and you wouldn't remember the next time. You get out Mrs. Rohr and go by her."

181

Laurel got the stained red volume down from the cupboard, and proceeded with the guidance of both Mrs. Rohr and Brindy. Miraculously, the cake rose. The chocolate icing was smooth and creamy. She bore her masterpiece to Chris's room for him to admire. The achievement was a sort of graduation. She suddenly felt that she could do anything.

With her new-found status, it seemed perfectly natural then when Rome said the next morning, "Come with me to the mill, Laurel, I want to pick up my paint things."

Gan, who was sitting at the desk writing a letter, looked up. "You must take Roy with you. He doesn't know what to do with himself while Chris is sick."

Roy was delighted when Rome allowed him to drive. Seated between them, he leaned forward, his feet barely touching the floor, and held a taut line in each hand. Rome smiled at her above his head. Infinitely older and wiser than her little brother, she was one with Rome.

When they reached the mill, Roy scampered off to wade in the ford, while Rome went into the mill. When he brought his things out, however, he did not take them to the buggy. Instead he set up the easel where he had had it before and placed the uncompleted canvas on it. Turning to her, he smiled disarmingly. "I have an idea. I think I'll put you in the picture."

"Me?" She had heard the words, but she could not believe them.

"Why not? It should have been you all along."

She could not move. It was a thing too wonderful to contemplate.

"Unbraid your hair," he said softly.

As though in a dream, she lifted her arms, untied the ribbons, began loosening her hair. She stopped. The pond? How could she?

Evidently he saw the alarm in her eyes. "I'm not suggesting that you pose in the water," he said quickly.

She was lying on the grass where Jenny had lain, and he

was bending over her just as he had bent over Jenny, arranging her hair. She looked up into his eyes, felt as though she could never pull her gaze away. "Laurel," he said, half under his breath, "you are the loveliest thing I ever saw."

Rome rose and went to the easel. "Shut your eyes," he said. She lay still, listening to the giant rushing of the water over the dam, feeling the solidity of the earth beneath her. She seemed a part of the earth, a part of the stream, a part of the tree above her. She was Laurel Carlton, but she was also earth and water and tree. She was life itself.

At last she stirred. An ant was voyaging over her arm.

"Don't move," Rome said.

The ant continued its exploration. She was not afraid of it, but it tickled. She longed to sit up, to smack it. A tiny spot on her nose began to itch. If she could only scratch it! How unthinkingly she had done just that a thousand times, yet never appreciated the opportunity. She discovered that her right leg had gone to sleep, had a terrible urgency to move it. "Rome," she said finally in a pleading voice, "I have to move."

"Not yet. In a few minutes."

Minutes, hours, ages, crept by. The roar of the water suddenly dwindled. In its place she could hear the muted hum of grinding in the mill. There was the metallic beat of horseshoes on stones as a team descended the slope to the ford. Then she felt the delicate vibration of bare running feet, and Roy was bending over her, crying, "Look, Laurel, look!" She opened her eyes to see a bullfrog dangling above her.

It was a beautiful green-backed frog, she noted, a fine catch. Many times she had tried to get her hands on one and never succeeded. "Good for you, Roy." She sat up for a better look.

"Really, Laurel!" Rome sounded angry. Then he added in a gentler tone, "You are completely unpredictable."

Apparently Roy became aware of something odd about

183

the situation. "Laurel, what are you doing lying on the ground with your hair all messed up?"

"I'm painting her picture," Rome explained. "But it must be about dinnertime. Here's some money. Run up to the store and get some cheese and crackers and whatever else looks good to you."

"Can I buy peppermint sticks and kisses?" Roy asked ecstatically.

"Sure."

Roy glanced down at the frog in his hands. "What'll I do with him?"

"If you put him down, I bet you a quarter he can't make it to the pond in one jump."

"A quarter?" Roy's eyes gleamed. He whirled about and set the frog down at a point from which he could not miss. One high arching leap, and he disappeared beneath the water. Rome handed Roy a quarter, and he ran off, calling over his shoulder that he was going to buy a jew's harp.

Laurel forgot to scratch her nose or kill the ant. "I—I'm sorry I moved," she said.

"I'll forgive you, angel. Just take that pose again." He came over to stoop down and arrange her hair as before. "How," he asked, "did you ever get so adorable?"

She lay suffused in bliss. He must love her or he would never have said that in just that tone. She relived the kiss he had given her on the drive home from the Crawleys'.

By the end of the week the picture was finished. Rome brought it home, set it up on the piano in the hall for all to view. Abashed, Laurel stood in a corner, her hands clasped behind her.

Edgar, leaning against the wall, his arms folded on his chest, said nothing, but he wore the suggestion of a scowl. She wasn't surprised. Lately he had been more moody than usual.

Gan's scrutiny lasted for some time. Finally she said, "It's well painted, Rome, but why do you always have to make

184

your pictures so tragic? Did she have to be drowned?"

Rome frowned. "If you want something dramatic, you've got to have contrast."

Jenny had stopped hemstitching a towel for her hope chest and was staring at the canvas, her eyes bright and hard, a flush on her cheeks.

Just then Uncle Walter came in through the back door, his blue shirt open at his throat, a film of red dust on his shoes. "What's all this?" His eyes went to the picture. "I'll be dadblamed, you've painted her dead. What's the sense in that, I'd like to know?"

He looked at Rome, and Laurel felt the live animosity running between them. An unreasoning expectancy filled her. They were going to fight again. For an instant, some deep primal thing in her gloated. Then she seemed to come back to herself, to the real Laurel Carlton that she usually was. And this self did not want them to fight, to hurt each other. This was the self that had jumped into the pond to stop that other fight.

Jenny turned on Walter. "I hope you're satisfied. He's painted Laurel instead of me. It's her picture that will go to New York and be hung in that show instead of mine."

Shocked silence filled the hall. Laurel looked at Jenny in disbelief. She had never heard anyone express envy as raw as that. How strange to be envied by Jenny, whom she herself had envied.

Uncle Walter's face turned dark red. "You bet I'm satisfied. No wife of mine is going to mess around with painters."

"I don't care what your wife does. She won't be me." Jenny jerked off her engagement ring, flung it at him, and rushed out of the hall.

185

chapter
21

JENNY PACKED her suitcase that night. Next morning the only question was who would take her to the train. She and Uncle Walter were not speaking; Edgar had to deliver some books; and Rome was remaining strictly neutral. Uncle Cam said he did not feel like driving such a pretty girl away from Blue Ridge View. It would have to be Billy, Gan said.

Laurel was genuinely shocked. Within her memory, no guest had left Blue Ridge View for the station at Pigeon Run without being accompanied by a member of the family.

Evidently, it was also too much for Uncle Walter. He said gruffly to Gan, "I'll drive the trap. Laurel can come."

"Very well."

Although she had little taste for the mission, Laurel set out with them, riding in the back seat with Jenny. Since the scene in the hall the day before, she'd had the uncomfortable feeling that Jenny regarded her as an enemy. There had been little conversation between them while Jenny packed, and in the night when she'd heard Jenny crying beside her in bed, she had not dared offer sympathy.

Billy, a ribald glint in his eyes, held open the big gate. A moment later the wheels were spinning over the road. The dusty hedgerows looked weary in the late August heat. But there was nothing weary about the tension in the surrey. Uncle Walter sat unnaturally erect in the middle of the front seat and concentrated on keeping the bays in step. He had chosen to wear both his hat and coat for the occasion, something he would normally have done in this weather for nothing less than a funeral.

Yet, in a sense, Laurel mused, this was a funeral.

At last Jenny apparently concluded that pride required her to talk. She began with a few scattered observations, speeding gradually up to her usual pace. But her words were addressed strictly to Laurel. "I certainly will be glad to get home," she kept repeating. "I certainly will be glad to see my folks. And I've got a lot to do."

At Cool Hill they met Mr. Allen, the mail carrier, but no one suggested stopping to see about the mail. Maybe he had a letter from Mother, Laurel thought. It was about time they heard again.

Jenny was saying, "It's time to make the watermelon pickle, and Mama says nobody can make the sweetmeats like me. Yes, indeed, I really do feel homesick. Just didn't know how homesick I was."

Laurel, realizing that her monologue was actually being delivered for the benefit of Uncle Walter, made only such monosyllabic replies as politeness required. She felt entirely superfluous. When they passed Tyler Morgan's blacksmith's shop, she had an impulse to get out and stay there watching

187

him shoe horses until Uncle Walter came back from the train. But conscience, plus a certain aloof curiosity, prevented her from suggesting it. As usual, Tyler paused to give them his hearty grin and wave his hat. Uncle Walter responded with a stiff gesture of the hand, and Jenny paid no attention at all.

White lather began to appear around the breeching and collars of Juno and Lady. Evidently taking note of this, Uncle Walter slowed them down.

The slackening of their speed seemed also to change the tempo of Jenny's speech. The underlying current of her thoughts was suddenly disclosed when she asked, "Laurel, how do you reckon your father and mother are going to like that picture? I bet they'll be mad."

Startled, and secretly disturbed, Laurel countered, "Why should they be mad?"

"For one thing, it's creepy. That old black millpond and you floating there like that. Did you get in the water by that log? That's one thing I certainly wouldn't do."

"No, he just let me lie on the bank where you were."

"Huh. That was bad enough with ants and things crawling all over you."

"You didn't seem to mind."

Jenny sniffed. "What do you know about it?"

"I know what I saw. You were willing enough until—" Annoyed as she was, she could not quite make herself finish.

"Go on and say it," Jenny cried. "Until Walter came rushing up like a mad dog. He was just jealous, that was all."

Suddenly Uncle Walter leaned over, jerked the whip out of the socket, and waved it over the horses, at the same time slapping the lines on their backs and yelling, "Get up there!"

The trap lurched forward. Juno and Lady broke into a lope. But even in his present state, he could not put up with that. He pulled them down to a trot.

Both Jenny and Laurel had grabbed the sides. "Never saw such driving," Jenny spluttered.

188

Laurel looked at Uncle Walter with renewed interest. What would he do next? Would he actually drive all the way to Pigeon Run without speaking? Ever since his attack on Rome, she had regarded him with wonder. How could somebody who was so matter-of-fact and down-to-earth make such a sudden change? Love must be the answer, but why should love have such a funny effect? For an instant, she looked inside herself. I haven't done anything funny, have I, not funny enough for people to notice? The answer was that people had noticed. But what had she done? She asked herself uneasily: Was it the way I looked at Rome?

At the idea the blood rushed hotly into her face. It was unbearable to think that other people could see through your face into your heart, that you could betray yourself. Because the thought was so disquieting, she thrust it away, and turned her attention once more to Uncle Walter and Jenny.

She decided to see whether he would speak to her. She leaned forward. "Uncle Walter, are you going to water the horses when you get to Pigeon Run?"

At first she thought he didn't intend to answer, then he said shortly, "A little. Can't give 'em their fill when they're hot."

Of course. She might have known what he'd say if he said anything.

Tilting her nose in the air, Jenny decided to make something of it. "Nothing like looking after your livestock. That's what's really important. When it comes to people now, it's a different thing. Treat them mean as you want to. That's where you work off your meanness."

Uncle Walter's ears went red, but he said nothing.

This seemed to spur Jenny on. "He's jealous," she declared loudly, "just plain jealous."

Her pink-and-white face was glowing, little sparkles of perspiration dotted her upper lip. She was sitting slightly forward, her eyes fixed on Uncle Walter's back. The daisies on her hat bobbed in time to the trotting horses.

Instinctively, Laurel knew that she was making a tactical error. Nobody liked to be called jealous, least of all somebody who was jealous. This, she concluded, was simply because you were afraid another person was loved better than you were. Of course Uncle Walter was wrong. There was nothing serious between Jenny and Rome. Not any more than there had been between Rome and Sylvia. But why had Rome acted as he had with them, why had he started things? The question was too painful for contemplation. She fought it down, recalled instead that drive home from the Crawleys', how it had been to have her head on his shoulder, to feel his lips on hers.

Jenny turned to her. "I can tell you one thing, Laurel, you'd better watch your step."

She didn't pretend to misunderstand. "If you'd done that yourself," she flared, "you wouldn't have had such a big row with Uncle Walter."

Again Uncle Walter urged the team forward, and they passed a wagon rattling along behind a pair of mules. They had already reached the colored village, which was only a little over a mile from Pigeon Run. The little whitewashed houses sat snugly back in a row beneath the oaks and hickories of the woods, and, except for children shouting and a dog or two barking, it was the picture of peace.

The peace did not extend to the surrey. "I don't know what you're talking about." Jenny's voice was shrill.

"You do, too. Reckon I saw you, didn't I?"

"Saw me? What do you mean by that?"

Laurel was silent. It hurt too much to go on. She couldn't bring herself to talk about how Jenny and Rome had looked at each other, how they had sat so close in the buggy.

Jenny leaned over and whispered in her ear. "You are jealous, aren't you?"

"I am not!"

"That's what I thought," Jenny said as though the denial

were a sort of affirmation. "I'm telling you for the last time you'd better stay away from him."

For an instant Laurel thought Uncle Walter was going to come to her defense, but he merely clucked to the horses. Her anger gave way to embarrassment. She felt exposed, alone. Because there had been concern rather than spite in Jenny's voice, it was hard to answer her.

They rounded a turn, could see the big store front of Odlum and Blount's two hundred yards away. Jenny glanced at the little watch pinned on her shirtwaist. "It's nearly time. I hope the train's not late."

Uncle Walter drove directly to the station, helped them out, and put Jenny's suitcase in the waiting room, then went to tie the horses in the shade.

Laurel watched Jenny buy her ticket, then sat down beside her on the wooden bench that was divided into separate compartments by iron arm rests. She liked the smell of coal smoke, the rattling of the telegraph keys. They were a prologue to the train, to Lynchburg, to New York—New York, which she had never seen, but which must be wonderful, if only because it was where Rome lived.

Alicia Parks came in, resplendent in her dimples and her blond beauty, carrying her music roll under her arm. She was rattling along to her pale older sister with all the casual sophistication of one accustomed to making the trip to Lynchburg every week. "Hello, Laurel," she said, "how are you, dear?" Not pausing for a reply, she moved on to the ticket window.

A stranger walked in wearing a derby hat and a checked suit, followed by two farmers, stiff in their Sunday clothes.

Instead of looking out of the window at the tracks, Jenny kept her eyes on the open door. Finally she got up. "Let's wait outside."

Laurel followed her, and they walked about, crunching the cinders under their feet. "Looks as if I'll have to carry my own suitcase," Jenny said.

Simultaneously, the train blew, and Uncle Walter appeared. Without a word, he strode into the waiting room and out again with the suitcase.

The ground was trembling beneath the approaching wheels. Jenny threw her arms around Laurel, kissed her tenderly. "Thanks, honey, for everything, for letting me stay in your room and all. Please write to me."

She was gone, assisted up the train steps by the conductor. Uncle Walter hadn't followed her, he had turned her suitcase over to the brakeman.

As the train pulled out, Laurel realized that Jenny had been crying. All the time she had been saying those sharp things in the surrey, she must have been crying inside.

When the train had disappeared into the distance, Uncle Walter touched her arm. "Wait in the trap," he said peremptorily, "got to get a few things at the store."

Later he drove to the watering trough and permitted the bays to drink lightly, then turned toward home. Slumped in his seat, he allowed Juno and Lady to take their time.

Laurel tried to put herself in his place and thus learn what he was thinking about, but found it quite impossible. Soon he would be returning to VPI for his last year in college. Would the thought of Jenny interfere with his studies, or would he go on just the same? He looked so grim, his mouth was so set, that it was hard to imagine any softness inside of him. Unable to restrain herself, she asked at last, "Are you going to be a bachelor now, Uncle Walter?"

He snorted. "Mind your own business, Missy."

chapter
22

WHEN THEY reached the Giffins' home, Mr. Giffin was pulling out into the road in his surrey. He waved them down. "Cablegram," he cried. "Mr. Wilkens just phoned it here. Was about to take it down to Mrs. Bowling."

Uncle Walter snapped to attention. "What does it say?"

" 'Arriving New York September 8th. John Carlton.' " He held out a slip of paper. "My wife wrote it down."

"Thanks." Uncle Walter shoved the paper into his pocket.

"Thought they were going to be away till the end of the month," Mr. Giffin said.

"Changed their plans." Uncle Walter gave the lines a quick shake.

As they drove on, Laurel noted Mr. Giffin's puzzled frown, saw Mrs. Giffin watching from a window.

"Oh," she burst out, "Mrs. Prickett sent it, she sent that cable!"

When she met Rome on the front porch, she had a terrible impulse to throw herself into his arms and cry. Instead, she wailed despairingly, "Oh, Rome, she sent it. They're coming home. Mother won't see Spain."

He seized her by the shoulder. "What's all this?"

She told him in little gasps.

Gan had come to the door. "Surely you are mistaken, Laurel, surely—"

"No," Uncle Walter said, "here's the message Mr. Giffin gave me." He handed her the slip of paper.

Fumbling as though to give herself time, she took her glasses out of her apron pocket and put them on. She read and re-read the few words. "Poor children," she said at last, "poor children."

"That woman," Rome said, "should be prosecuted."

Uncle Walter stepped toward him. "It's as much your fault as hers."

"You lie."

Uncle Walter raised his fist. Gan moved between them. "Please, boys, don't make matters any worse."

Slowly Uncle Walter's arm fell.

"Yes," Rome said grimly, "we might at least pretend to be civilized."

Gan was looking at the message again. "It's from Florence," she said. "No address. No mention of what port or what ship. We can't reach them."

Mrs. Prickett's bell jangled querulously.

"Laurel," Gan said, "please see what she wants."

Mrs. Prickett leaned forward from her mound of pillows, her face flushed, her spectacles gleaming. "What's going on out there?"

Laurel trembled with rage. "You sent that cable!"

194

"Are they coming home?" Mrs. Prickett's tone was exultant.

"Who sent that cable for you?"

"It's none of your business, but I don't care who knows. I wrote my son, he did it."

"How could you?" Laurel's voice broke. "You've ruined everything."

"On the contrary, I may have saved the day. They are coming, aren't they?"

Laurel did not answer. In the hall she found Gan sitting in the armchair near the door, still holding the slip of paper. "They must be so worried," she said sadly. "I'd give anything if I could have saved them from this." Laurel had never seen her so defeated looking.

Mrs. Prickett called out loudly, "Mrs. Bowling, when will they get here?"

Uncle Walter strode to her open door. "Shut up," he told her, "before I forget you're a woman with a broken leg."

Mrs. Prickett seemed to know better than to answer.

Rome paced up and down the hall frowning to himself. Laurel watched him uneasily. What was he thinking? He seemed to have forgotten her completely.

It was at supper that evening that the next blow fell. Turning to Gan, Rome said, "I should be getting back to New York Monday, Aunt Celia."

Laurel sagged in her chair. Her fork fell from her hand. She couldn't move or speak.

"Can't you wait to see Margaret and John?" Gan asked.

"I'm afraid not. Crayton wants me to get back so he can have my new pictures framed for the show. It's been a wonderful summer. I really think I have accomplished something."

Uncle Walter gave a snort.

Edgar's face lighted. "Gee whiz, Rome. Hadn't figured you were going that soon. But I'll be ready."

Rome cleared his throat. "Don't want you to rush, fellow,

I know you have your sales work to do. Why don't we make it next summer?"

For a moment, Edgar just looked at him. Then he pushed back his chair, jumped up, and ran out of the room. They heard the slamming of the back door.

Gan looked reproachfully at Rome. "Didn't you promise to take him to New York?"

"Oh, we talked about it. Don't remember that we set a definite date."

Her expression was grave. "He understood that it was to be this fall. He's been counting on it."

Laurel stared at Rome in shocked disbelief. Her whole body down to the remotest cell refused to accept the statement that he was leaving. She was not thinking about Edgar, or Edgar's disappointment; she was thinking only that if Rome left, she would die.

Somehow the meal ended. She saw him go out into the yard, followed at a distance. She did not know what she was going to say or do, she wanted only to be near him.

He was standing in the shadow of the boxwoods. She stopped at a little distance, stood mute. Somewhere in the twilight a tree frog signaled the advent of fall. The familiar sound was fatalistic. It meant the end of summer, the end of everything.

"Laurel." Rome came toward her, holding out his hand. Without a word, she put her hand in his. They moved toward the garden gate. "Fall is in the air," he said. "I noticed it for the first time."

Through dry lips she managed to ask, "Do you have to go?"

They were through the gate now, standing in a shadowy archway of the boxwoods. He put his hands on her shoulders, gazed intently into her face. "Don't you want me to go?"

She could not answer. Instead, she did something that she had never dreamed she would do in his presence, she burst into tears. Then her face was against his breast, his arms were

196

holding her close.

They stood there like that, she could not guess how long, she only wanted it to be forever. At last he released her. Above the wild beating of her heart, she could hear the quick, uneven sound of his breathing. "I should have left sooner," he said. "I knew I should."

"No, oh, no."

"I knew I shouldn't touch you; I knew you were forbidden." It seemed as though he were talking to himself.

"Laurel!" Suddenly she was in his arms again. In the midst of her happiness, she felt a tiny twinge of fear. And then the fear was forgotten.

When he released her again, he whispered, "Go with me back to New York."

She jumped. To New York? With him? It was beyond thinking. "I'd rather have you stay here," she said.

"You know I can't do that. Will you go with me?"

"They would never let me."

"We'll have to run away, my darling."

She was trembling.

He went on, "Since I told them I was leaving Monday, they won't be surprised to see me packing. But you and I will leave Sunday night. We'll get the early morning train at Pigeon Run that goes south. We can get off at the first stop, and take the next train north. They won't know where we are."

chapter
23

SUNDAY. LAUREL'S last day at home. She couldn't believe it. She seemed to be floating through reality like a fish in clear water. She could see the pebbles, the gray boulders, the tree roots, the other fish, but there was something between—the strange continuum of the water. In church she sat beside Gan, unable to listen to the sermon.

Through the windows on the right she could see the weathered old Masonic Lodge surrounded by oak trees. The horse and buggy belonging to Mr. Fairlea, the Sunday-school superintendent, waited in the shade. Since his wife had eczema on her face and seldom went out, he usually rode horseback. But today he had brought his daughter, Anita, who was at home on vacation from her secretarial job in Roanoke. Anita's beauty was recognized by all, and the year before she had won the cake for the prettiest girl at the church lawn party.

Laurel glanced toward her now, sitting by her father just across the aisle. In contrast to the other girls, Anita looked pale, and her face had an almost classical perfection. It made Laurel think of a piece of exquisite sculpture. The sheer violet organdy matched her eyes, and her black hair gleamed beneath her picture hat. But her charms had never made her vain, and she maintained a simple natural warmth toward her family and her former neighbors. In brief, Laurel could see no flaw in her, and her admiration had always been tinged with envy.

But today she could even be tolerant of another girl's beauty. After all she had Rome, and Rome found her desirable. Nothing else mattered.

Her eyes wandered on to a window on the left through which she could see the red line of the road cutting through the landscape toward home. When she took that road in the surrey with the others, it would be for the last time.

Leaning a little forward, she looked at Rome, who sat on the other side of Gan. Though he did not always come to church, he had chosen to do so today. In his dark suit, he was perfectly groomed, and she had never seen him look more handsome. She felt a surge of pride that was almost unbearable. At the same time she experienced a wonderful sense of unity. Their secret made them one. Somehow the presence of the congregation served only to intensify this unity.

But Rome's head was turned the other way. Following his gaze, she saw that it was fixed on Anita. At first it was only a fact. The chill came later, a chill that stabbed her like an icicle. Anita caught his eye and flushed. He gave a nod that was scarcely perceptible. It seemed to say, "Yes, you are beautiful, and I know it."

Just then a hymn was announced, and as they all rose,

Anita's gloves fell into the aisle. Instantly Rome glided forward, picked them up, and gave them to her with a little bow. The incident was over; the service proceeded.

Laurel remained stunned. Then slowly she began to take herself in hand. She was just being silly. After all everybody admired Anita. Why shouldn't Rome? Admiration was one thing, and love was another. And he loved her, Laurel. Didn't he? The question was so absurd that she refused to answer it. Hadn't he asked her to go to New York with him? Weren't they running away tonight?

On the drive home she sat in the back seat of the surrey between Rome and Gan. The pressure of Rome's arm against hers reassured her. Once more she felt a warm surge of happiness throughout her body. She relaxed against his shoulder, filled with the poignant sadness that accompanies last things. Last visits, last journeys, last goodbyes. Summer was dying along the hedgerows. Dust powdered the goldenrod, the little wild grapes, the dark red bunches of sumac. Already the poison ivy and sweet gum leaves were beginning to turn red and gold. Inevitably, fall was coming, then winter.

Edgar galloped past on Byron, gave them a single dark glance.

Gan turned to Rome. "I have done all of Edgar's mending. Have you told him what to pack?"

Rome cleared his throat. "No, Aunt Celia. As I said the other night, it would be better for him to wait till next year."

"But he has already waited so long. Please don't disappoint him again."

Uncle Walter turned around in the front seat, where he sat driving with Chris and Roy beside him. The look he gave Rome did not need words to back it up.

Rome's attention was on Gan. Laurel sensed a struggle going on within him. "I am sorry," he said. "Someday I'll make it up to him."

Gazing full into his eyes, Laurel caught something unfamiliar in their depths. Unfamiliar, yet oddly revealing. She recalled the fairy story about a pixie imprisoned in an opal. He could only writhe about in eternal defiance of the forces that held him there. Was Rome like that pixie, forever battling against something in his own nature that would not let him be? He needed help, he needed her. She was seized with a nameless compassion.

The hooves of the horses struck the planks of the bridge. Involuntarily she glanced up at the cliff. Was she seeing it for the last time?

Under the bridge roof the steel shoes of the horses beat out an echoing finale. The creek, she thought, the bathing hole, she would be giving up all that. The idea filled her with luxurious melancholy.

Before them rose the familiar red hill. Sir Julian was scouting intently through the stubble of a wheat field, anticipating no doubt the hunting season that would soon begin. She thought of the ecstasy with which he leaped about when Papa got down his shotgun and put on his brown corduroy hunting coat. At night they would come home weary and content. Limply, Sir Julian would stretch out before the fire in the dining room, and not move until he was called to supper.

The silence in the surrey was broken only by the chatter of Chris and Roy. She felt a surge of thankfulness that Chris was able to chatter. Gan, having made her plea, had nothing more to say.

Seeking further reassurance, Laurel glanced again at Rome. His eyes were warm and embracing. All for her. All for her? Only a short while ago he had looked at Anita. In spite of herself, she recalled the intensity of that look. Again she tried to argue that everyone admired Anita, that Rome should not be blamed. Then, relentlessly, her thoughts went back to Sylvia and Jenny. But surely they could have meant nothing to him. Not any more than Anita did. It was she, Laurel, whom he really loved.

Resolutely she choked down her questions and concentrated on their plan. Rome had said it would be better for her to go through the field and meet him at the top of Oak Tree Hill. Meantime, he would quietly take his baggage down to the stable and hitch Lady to the buggy.

That Sunday afternoon was the longest that she could remember. Not once was she alone with Rome, who spent most of the time in his room packing. As for her own packing, it was already done. Rome had told her not to take much since he would buy her suitable clothes in New York. Into the suitcase that Papa had bought her when she visited a cousin the summer before, she had put her toilet articles, a few underthings, and the green velvet dress that Mother had made for best last winter. She would wear her dark blue organdy and the straw sailor hat with the blue ribbon. The money in her china bank amounted to three dollars and eighty-five cents.

Uncle Walter sat at the desk in the hall writing a letter. He wrote slowly, setting down a few words at a time, then pausing to harrow through his hair with his work-toughened fingers. Once Gan glanced up from the *Christian Advocate* she was reading, nodded to herself, and turned back to the paper. In a flash, Laurel understood, it must be a letter to Jenny. Remembering Jenny's tears, she could not doubt the outcome. In a surge of munificence, she wished for their happiness. Her own would be so great that there would be plenty to spare.

Had Mrs. Prickett's bell rung at the moment, she could even have answered that summons with grace. But the bell did not ring so often any more. Following Uncle Walter's explosion, and a subsequent visit from Gan, she had seemed somewhat subdued. Passing her door now, Laurel saw her holding the open Bible. Was she looking for justification? In any case, Mrs. Prickett no longer seemed important.

In the front yard, Laurel felt the dry brown grass crackle beneath her feet. Without having taken on the gay tints of autumn, some leaves from the cutleaf maple had fallen. Drifts of wilted leaves lay under the locust trees in the triangle. We need rain, she thought, remembering the pleasant sound it made on the shingle roof. But she would not hear it again in her room here at Blue Ridge View.

As though from a great distance, she saw Edgar lying in the hammock, his arms folded behind his head, his eyes blank and staring. If he noticed her, he said nothing.

She went through the lilac hedge to find Uncle Cam dozing in the rocking chair beside his door. His mouth was open, and he snored gently. But she felt no temptation to sprinkle salt or soda on his tongue. It was another Laurel who had indulged in tricks like that. Not this Laurel, who was planning this very night to run away with her lover.

Uncle Cam gave an unexpected snort and opened his eyes. "Now don't ask me to go to the creek," he grumbled. "I don't feel able."

"I don't want to go to the creek," she said loftily.

"Hah, you don't?" His tone was suspicious. "Then what are you up to?"

"Nothing."

He regarded her doubtfully. "You been moping around lately. I'll be bound you're up to something."

She became still, watchful. "What?" she asked.

"Good gracious, how do I know? You've done so many things."

She concluded that he had no idea of the truth. How could he? On an impulse, she bent and kissed his cheek. "I love you, Uncle Camee."

She retrieved his book from the ground and continued on to the kitchen. Brindy was just leaving, a pan of food in her hand. "Where you going?" Brindy's question was casual.

"Nowhere."

Feeling an obscure desire to say something that couldn't be said, Laurel walked beside her across the woodpile. Brindy wouldn't be back for supper, this was the last time she would see her. She was thinking of the secret tray Brindy had brought to her upstairs, of all the times she had given her special things from the kitchen, tea cakes, chicken livers, a rare cup of cocoanut milk. But you couldn't say thank you for things like that in a lump sum. At last she managed, "After the way Mrs. Prickett did you, it was nice of you to come back and stay."

"It wasn't her I was thinking about, it was Mrs. Bowling." She paused. "Seems like that cable Mrs. Prickett sent is rousting folks out."

"What do you mean by that?"

"Don't act like you don't know." She stopped and eyed Laurel speculatively. "Reckon maybe it's time for Mr. John and Miss Margaret to be getting back."

Laurel watched her go down the path. What was on her mind? Brindy didn't miss much. But she could have been thinking of the affair with Sylvia, the quarrel over Jenny. Whatever she knew, she couldn't know what was going to happen tonight. Only she and Rome knew that.

In the hall after supper, she did not dare meet his eyes. Such a glance would say too much, it might be intercepted, understood. Sitting in a corner, silent, she had strange contradictory emotions. On the one hand, she longed for time to pass, for the moment to come when she would get into the buggy with Rome and drive away. On the other hand, she wanted the evening to last. She wanted to remember how everything was. Gan's silver hair shone in the lamp light as she watched Rome divide the change in his pockets between Chris and Roy. Uncle Walter was discussing horses with Uncle Cam. Edgar was nowhere in sight.

Now and then the lonely sound of the tree frogs floated in through the open door. But the foreshadowing of autumn could not bring gloom. This autumn would be different. It would not be an ending, but a beginning. A shiver of anticipation ran through her.

Happy with their treasure, Roy and Chris were sent to bed. Gan went to the piano and played a few hymns.

Then quite suddenly, the evening was over. It was bedtime for all. When Gan kissed her, Laurel astonished herself by almost bursting into tears. Hurriedly she left the hall, ran for the last time up the crooked stairs to her room. There on her bureau she had taken the precaution of placing the alarm clock from the kitchen—not that she would need the alarm, she merely wanted to know the time. Tonight she would not go to bed. She dressed herself in the blue organdy and put on her hat. Then she pulled out her suitcase from under the bed and laid her purse on it.

There was still a lot of time. She took down a copy of *David Copperfield* from the row of books on the mantelpiece and began rereading favorite parts. Somehow she was always sorry for Steerforth. Though he was supposed to be the villain, he did not really seem like one. She came to the passage where he asked to be remembered at his best. That, she mused, would be a wonderful thing for everybody. People needed to be thought of at their best. After all, it was a part of them.

How still the house was at midnight, still, yet somehow alive. You could hear tiny creaks and movements in the walls and floors. Now that its occupants had retired, it seemed to awaken and enjoy the freedom of being itself. She felt awed, but not afraid.

At last the time came. Returning the book to its place, she picked up her suitcase and purse, blew out the lamp. Her heart was beating so hard that it shook her whole body. To make it quiet down, she pushed her fist against it.

Since doors at Blue Ridge View were never locked, and in summer rarely closed, she crept down the stairs and out onto the back porch with scarcely a sound. But Sir Julian was aware of her presence. Tapping his tail in greeting, he rose to follow her. Unaccountably glad of his company, she stroked his head.

As she crossed the lane near the well, she thought she heard the stable door open. So Rome, too, had gotten out successfully. She pushed her suitcase under the barbed wire fence, then carefully lifted a strand and got through herself. With Sir Julian trotting beside her, she passed through the dim hay field. At every step, her heart throbbed more wildly. She felt breathless, choked, as if she couldn't speak if she had to.

The oak tree loomed ahead of her. A bramble caught in one stocking. She pulled it away, kept on. Now she had reached the tree, crawled under the fence. She stood beside the road with her suitcase. Sir Julian, plainly aware that the whole thing was unusual, sat on his haunches close beside her, licking her hand.

When she first heard the wheels, she jumped involuntarily. At a crest of excitement, even the expected could be a surprise. There was the tapping of hooves on the small wooden bridge at the foot of Oak Tree Hill. In another minute, Rome would be there. Her heart was beating louder than the hooves. It was in her throat, her mouth, it was suffocating her.

Up the hill, up the hill! The buggy was coming up the hill. Rome, oh, Rome! He was there, right in front of her. He had stopped.

She stood motionless.

"Laurel?"

She could see the white blur of his face. He would leap out now, take her suitcase, help her in. But he remained where he was. "Laurel?" he repeated, and there was something strange in his tone.

"Yes," she answered, "I'm all ready."

"Darling. How can I say it?"

"Say what?" she asked in sudden fear.

"What I have to say, Laurel. You know I love you, I want you. But now that the time has come, I can't do it—I can't take you away from here."

She heard the words, but they did not make sense. She took a step forward. "Rome, let me get in. Please help me. I—I have my suitcase."

He leaned down, touched her cheek. "Someday you'll understand and thank me." He added in his everyday voice, "Tell Billy I'll leave the horse with Mr. Odlum."

Before she could answer or move, he had spoken to Lady, the wheels began to turn. Faster, faster, faster.

For a long time, she stood where she was, perfectly still, holding the suitcase. "Rome," she cried despairingly, "Rome, Rome!"

There was only the fading answer of wheels and hooves. She was unable to believe what had happened.

Sir Julian whimpered, and thrust his nose against her hand. He was right, of course, she couldn't stay there by the road. Slowly, dragging her suitcase with her, she crawled back under the fence into the hay field. There she threw herself, face down, on the ground and began to cry. She cried like a child in loud, uninhibited wails that echoed through the quiet night. She cried like that until she was exhausted, until her face sank into the grass, and intermittent gasping sobs were muted by the earth.

For a while, Sir Julian circled around, then at last he lay down beside her and lapsed into a dog doze.

The eerie voice of an owl came from somewhere, perhaps the oak tree. It was the voice of loneliness, a terrible loneliness that gripped and held her closer than the night. Finally, the sobs ceased. Spent and inert, she lay there staring into the darkness. And gradually her mind began to function again. The truth that she had refused to recognize forced its way into her consciousness. It was simple, inescapable, and utterly devastating. Rome did not love her, he had never loved her.

At last it began to grow light. Over the woods to the East appeared the red edge of the sun. Deep within her, something stirred with the light. She had to move. She sat up, gazed toward Blue Ridge View. Home. But she couldn't go there. Not now.

She looked toward the familiar woods in the northwest

beyond the dewberry field. There she would be hidden. Leaving her suitcase, her hat, her purse, in a forlorn heap, she set out. Sir Julian waltzed ahead, assuming a mood of gaiety that he evidently hoped would infect her, too.

She crossed the fields and the branch, unmindful of the ruin of her silk stockings, the scratches on her legs, the tears in her dress. She reached the dewberry patch, now only a tangle of briars and weeds. The hot red sun was hanging above the horizon when she got to the woods, plunged into the cool and welcome shade. She paused to get her breath, leaned against a tree trunk. A cottontail flashed by, Sir Julian in pursuit.

She walked on again, going instinctively toward Sheep Rock. But she did not approach it with the old feeling of anticipation and excitement, she walked as though in sleep. At last she reached it, ascended the slope to the top, to the precipitous edge. Feeling no fear, she sat down, her legs swinging over the abyss. There was relief in the sensation of danger. She gazed down the gray wall at the water rushing over the stones, began to feel the spell of the subtle invitation. She bent farther, farther, unafraid, drawn.

"Laurel!"

She turned with the fuzzy bewildered consciousness of one suddenly awakened. Edgar was striding toward her. "What do you think you're doing?"

She couldn't answer.

He came on, seized her by the shoulders, dragged her back from the edge. "Are you crazy?" he demanded gruffly.

But his tone was not matched by the look in his eyes. In their depths, she recognized something new, something she had never seen in them before. "You followed me," she accused faintly.

"Your face is dirty," he said. "You look a mess." He smoothed the hair back from her forehead, and she thought with wonder that nobody had ever touched her with greater tenderness.